"You think since you stayed overnight I should let you move in?"

Derek's words infuriated her. Macey took a slow, calming breath that actually didn't do a damn thing to settle her. Her head throbbed in time with her pulse.

"I don't want anything *from* you," she finally answered. "I want something *for* you. Something like peace of mind. Your old personality. A flash of happiness now and then. That's all I want, Derek. Forgive me for cleaning. I was trying to be nice, but that seems to be a foreign concept to you."

"I didn't ask you to be nice. Matter of fact, I made it very clear I wasn't up for a visit when you came to town."

Fine. She got his message. Blindly, she grabbed her purse and hurried down the hall to the door.

"Macey... Wait."

Dear Reader,

When I first started writing *Playing with Fire,* it centered on a little beach bar in Texas, but there were no firefighters. The hero, Derek Severson, kept trying to get through to me, though. Kept insisting that while he currently managed the bar, he used to be a firefighter. I tried to shut him up—tried to tell him the bar was enough—but in the end, Derek was right. He was a firefighter before fleeing to San Amaro Island to manage the Shell Shack.

Of course I've always looked up to firefighters and the job they do, but delving further into their world, researching what they do on a daily basis, has grown my admiration for them immensely. They're true heroes, through and through.

Even though Derek is grieving a recent tragedy, and mixing drinks for a living, he's still that hero deep inside. Still the kind of man to put others first, to drop everything to rescue someone in need.

Now his best friend, Macey Locke, has to turn the tables and rescue the brooding firefighter. Because she's known for years that Derek is the perfect man for her.

Thank you for picking up Derek and Macey's story. I hope you enjoy reading it as much as I enjoyed writing it. I love to hear from readers, so please feel free to stop by my Web site, www.amyknupp.com, my blog, www.writemindedblog.com, or contact me directly at amyknupp@amyknupp.com.

Amy Knupp

Playing with Fire
Amy Knupp

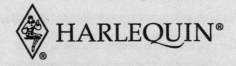

HARLEQUIN®

TORONTO • NEW YORK • LONDON
AMSTERDAM • PARIS • SYDNEY • HAMBURG
STOCKHOLM • ATHENS • TOKYO • MILAN • MADRID
PRAGUE • WARSAW • BUDAPEST • AUCKLAND

Recycling programs
for this product may
not exist in your area.

ISBN-13: 978-0-373-71646-3

PLAYING WITH FIRE

ABOUT THE AUTHOR

Amy Knupp lives in Wisconsin with her husband, two sons and five (feline) beasts. She graduated from the University of Kansas with degrees in French and journalism and feels lucky to use very little of either one in her writing career. She's a member of Romance Writers of America and shares a blog with four other published authors, called Writeminded. In her spare time, she enjoys reading, college basketball, addictive computer games and watching big red fire trucks race by. To learn more about Amy and her writing, visit www.amyknupp.com.

Books by Amy Knupp

HARLEQUIN SUPERROMANCE

1342—UNEXPECTED COMPLICATION
1402—THE BOY NEXT DOOR
1463—DOCTOR IN HER HOUSE
1537—THE SECRET SHE KEPT

Don't miss any of our special offers. Write to us at the following address for information on our newest releases.

Harlequin Reader Service
U.S.: 3010 Walden Ave., P.O. Box 1325, Buffalo, NY 14269
Canadian: P.O. Box 609, Fort Erie, Ont. L2A 5X3

Dedicated to Mary Ann, my aunt who read
each of my books and always e-mailed me
to tell me her favorite details.
I wish she had lived long enough to read this story.
I think she would've been amused with
the vintage 70s block-and-a-half-long, dent- and
personality-filled Lincoln named after her.

Acknowledgments

To the retired firefighter (in typical hero style,
he asked to not be recognized) who's been amazingly
patient and thorough in his answers to my
never-ending questions. Without his generous help,
I couldn't have written this book or the two that follow
in the trilogy. Any errors or inaccuracies regarding
firefighting are entirely mine. Thank you many times
over…and that still doesn't seem sufficient.

To the members of the Writeminded Readers Group…
You've been cheering for my firefighters since before
the stories were even contracted. Thank you for your
enthusiasm, your encouragement and your friendship.

To my family… My mom and dad for supporting me
and shamelessly promoting me to everyone they know.
My boys for doing their best to keep tabs on how
many books I've written, which one I'm working on
and what the title will be. My husband for believing in
me and giving me the opportunity to chase my dreams
full-time. Thank you all for dealing with Amy On
Deadline and loving me anyway.

CHAPTER ONE

MACEY LOCKE DIDN'T OFTEN wake up alone in a man's bed. She didn't often wake up in a man's bed *period*. But here she was, sprawled across Derek Severson's mattress, hogging the covers, hugging the pillow.

Fantastic. An awkward "morning after" and she hadn't even had the pleasure of spending the night with him.

Not that that would happen. Not now, not ever.

She sat up, cringing as she recalled the night before. She'd driven all day to get to Derek's bar on San Amaro Island, and though she'd tried to prepare herself for the state he was in, his less-than-enthusiastic reception had cut deep. She'd stupidly thought just the sight of an old friend—*her*—would dig through his layers of grief and sorrow and at least warrant a smile.

She'd thought wrong.

Macey helped herself to the connecting bathroom and splashed water on her face, then looked longingly at the tiny shower stall. Maybe later. She'd made herself at home enough already, barging in and stealing his bed while he closed up the bar. That she'd never intended to fall asleep didn't make it any more acceptable.

She ran a brush through her hair and pulled it up into a sloppy bun as she returned to the bedroom. Her flip-flops were next to the bed, where her feet had been hanging over the side; she must've kicked them off in her sleep. She slipped them on, and was about to go find Derek when she noticed the framed photo she'd left among the pile of blankets. Once again she was compelled to pick it up.

Julie. Derek's girlfriend who'd died.

She'd known Julie vaguely. Had watched as Derek fell in love with her. It was part of what had pushed Macey to do something as drastic as joining the Peace Corps two years ago.

But instead of the cutting jealousy she'd felt toward this woman, now sorrow made her throat burn and her eyes water anew.

Feeling even more like an intruder, she set the photo back on the nightstand and left the room, wiping tears away.

Had Derek even bothered to come home?

The soft drone of the television answered her question as she reached the open kitchen and living area. There he was. Crashed out on a worn, once overstuffed chair that looked too small for his long, muscled body to be anything close to comfortable. He was still asleep. She should give him privacy but...

Wow.

He wore a pair of black boxers, nothing else. A large tattoo of the Texas Longhorn logo, with flames added behind it, emphasized the size of his biceps. His chest was sculpted with muscles and a sprinkling of light-colored hair trailing down the most ripped abs she'd ever seen. She'd thought six-pack abs were fictional, but they were totally alive and oh-so-well here. Her eyes tracked slowly, appreciatively downward and eventually landed on strong, solid thighs. She swallowed hard, knowing this little inspection of hers was a really bad idea for a girl who couldn't afford to be attracted to this man. She watched his chest rise and fall for a few breaths before her gaze traveled up to his face.

That was like having a bucket of cold water poured over her head. Derek looked exhausted, as if he hadn't slept for a month. The hair on his chin was more than a shadow, making him appear older, rougher than he was. His ash-blond hair was longer than she'd ever seen it; for Derek, normally with military-short hair, that meant maybe long enough for a woman to run her fingers through it. She clenched her hands into fists.

Macey recalled the emptiness in his eyes last night, and she ached to comfort him somehow. To touch him, to run her palms gently down his arms, to hold his hands in hers.

Derek would never tolerate her sympathy, though.

What he'd have to figure out was that she was no longer the shy, afraid-of-confrontation girl he'd known. The Peace Corps had changed her in so many ways, and she wasn't going to back down from him, tough firefighter or not, no matter how ugly he got with her.

Derek stirred in the chair, turned his head the other way, and she waited for him to discover her admiring him. But his eyes remained closed, and he exhaled deeply before slipping back into even breathing.

Macey stepped away silently, filled with so many emotions her head felt as if it would burst.

She belatedly noticed the view out the sliding-glass door and the mostly glass wall. Waves. Sand. Patches of sea grass. Lots of people. She unlatched the door, glancing toward Derek to make sure he was still asleep. She needed to get her head straight before round two with him, so she slid the door open without a sound and went out.

AS SOON AS MACEY WAS GONE, Derek got up to deal with the kink in his neck, stomping his left foot to wake his leg. Feigning sleep had been nearly impossible because of his discomfort, but the last thing he could handle was a cheery morning greeting from Macey.

Damn woman. What was she doing here?

He checked out the door and spotted her light brown hair and short frame halfway between the patio and the waves. Last night at the bar, there'd been a moment when he'd been glad to see her. Had perked up when she'd appeared. He'd tamped that down right away, though. He didn't want to hurt Macey, but dammit, he'd come as far south as he could—while still being in Texas—to be by himself.

After throwing on clothes, he strode to the kitchen and turned on his cell phone. Ignoring the display that told him he had twelve messages, he punched in his mother's number.

"Hello?"

"I don't need a babysitter, Mom. I'm twenty-eight years old."

"Derek, it's good to hear your voice. You've been ignoring my calls."

"Running a bar here. Tell Macey she can go back home. I don't want her around."

"I'm not going to tell Macey anything. I'm not—"

"Cut the crap, Mom. I know you put her up to it." He paced through the condo blindly. "Look, I know you're trying to help. What I need right now is to be alone."

"You can't mean that. Maybe Macey's exactly what you need. She won't push you—"

"Damn right, she won't, because she can't stay here."

"You'll have to take that up with her. She's planned a six-week vacation for herself down there. Well-deserved after spending two years in Thailand, wouldn't you say?"

Derek ground his teeth together. He loved his mom—he really did. But there was a reason he hadn't returned her calls. Hell, there was a reason he'd jumped at the chance to move away and run Gus's bar for him. This kind of call was that reason, clearly and emphatically.

"Gotta go, Mom. Goodbye." He ended the call and set the phone down hard on the counter.

At an unobtrusive knock on the glass door, he whipped around, ready to blow. Of course, it was Macey. He couldn't ignore her, as he would a stranger, and that just pissed him off more. He went to the door and slid it open, his frustration thinly veiled.

"I hope I didn't wake you," she said, eyeing him carefully.

"No. Look, Mace—"

"I just need to borrow your sink. Maybe a bandage if you have one."

He followed her gaze downward and noticed she wasn't putting any weight on her left foot. She lifted it to the side to reveal blood on the sand.

"What happened?" Grudgingly, he let her inside.

"Sliced it on a rock. I'm fine." She hopped to the kitchen and looked around. "Paper towels?"

"Don't have any. Here." He picked her up—she weighed next to nothing—and put her on the counter next to the sink.

"Derek!"

"Let me look." He grasped her slender calf and she stiffened.

"I can take care of it," she said quietly but firmly. "All I need is some kind of…rag."

"I'll get you some toilet paper and a bandage if you sit still."

Their eyes met in a standoff. After several seconds, she nodded in acquiescence and he went to the hall bath.

"Let me make sure there's no sand rubbed into the cut." He didn't ask and he didn't make eye contact; he just went for her leg again, and this time she let him.

"Well?" she asked.

"There's sand. We'll run water over it to clean it."

DEREK HAD CHANGED, Macey thought as she watched him. Even more than she'd expected.

She wanted nothing more than to give him the space he craved, but that wasn't why she was here. And okay, it wasn't entirely the truth, either.

The truth was she'd do just about anything to help him stop hurting so much.

She studied the angry set of his jaw as he carefully, tenderly rinsed her foot in the sink. His mom had cautioned her he would be difficult. Macey had tried to prepare herself for it, had come down here of her own accord in spite of Mrs. Severson's warnings. She was beginning to understand now.

The man he'd been was still in there somewhere, though, buried deep. His insistence on seeing to her injury was all the proof she needed. Derek had always been one to watch out for her, to help anyone in need. Helping was his nature as much as hers was to bring order to things. The trick would be to get to that inner Derek, the one she'd known and loved for so many years. To pull him out.

"I'm sorry I stole your bed last night," she said.

"No big deal." He continued to scowl as he worked on her foot.

"I must have been exhausted to fall asleep like that."

"Long drive," he said shortly.

"Anyway, thanks for letting me stay there. I slept like the...like a baby."

"You can say 'dead.' Avoiding the word doesn't change that she is."

"I'm...sorry, Dare," Macey said quietly. "That she died. I never got to say that."

He met her gaze finally, just for an instant, and in that moment she saw so much pain she reached out to him. Touched his shoulder.

He stood abruptly. "Wound is cleaned and bandaged. I'm going on a run before work."

Before she could slide off the counter, he was gone.

CHAPTER TWO

WHEN MACEY WALKED UP to The Shell Shack—Derek's thatch-roofed, open-air bar on the beach—a couple of hours later, she couldn't help but notice he was oblivious to the woman he was taking an order from. That was saying a lot, as she was endowed enough for two people and apparently took pride in showing off her good fortune with a teeny string bikini top. She wore a barely there sarong on the bottom that revealed to-die-for legs, and Macey instantly felt like the short, plain girl she'd always been. Her own thin-strapped tank and short denim skirt were about as daring and sexy as her wardrobe got.

Macey stood in line behind four or five people to order some lunch. The menu consisted of a few simple items like shrimp, nachos, burgers and hot dogs, she noted. And then she realized there were more people gathered all the way around the bar, waiting to order. Derek was by himself behind the counter, although she could see a woman in the small kitchen in back, zipping around, preparing food.

After fifteen minutes Macey had hardly advanced, and wasn't any closer to ordering. Derek still appeared to be calm, but he was starting to get impatient comments from people in line. The day was hot and humid already, and she could see sweat forming along his hairline.

He was never going to wait on everyone by himself.

Macey watched him for several more minutes before jumping into action. She slipped around the end of the counter and fumbled around until she found a pad of paper. She spotted a pen by the cash register, then went to the side opposite Derek and took an order.

As she reached into the beer cooler, Derek came up behind her.

"What are you doing?"

He sounded pissed off instead of grateful for her help.

"Saving your butt." Sweet butt that it was.

She took out three bottles and walked away, not looking back to gauge his reaction. She snatched one of the flimsy paper menus as a price guide and went to the cash register to ring up the order. Thankfully, the machine was old and straightforward.

The second group ordered Bloody Marys and shrimp, which presented a double problem. Macey went to the back room and quickly took in the sight of the slender girl in her mid-twenties pressing burgers on the grill.

"Who're you?" the leggy brunette asked.

"A friend of Derek's. He's getting slammed out there. Do I give you food orders?"

The girl took the piece of paper from Macey and set it on the counter in answer. *Ooo-kay.* She'd take that as a yes. Now she just needed to figure out how to make a Bloody Mary. She returned to the front.

She knew there was tomato juice in them, so she searched for a can of it. The place was a disaster area, as Derek flew around mixing, stirring, adding this and that. Macey stepped next to him.

"Bloody Marys," she said, speaking loudly to be heard over the chatter.

Derek looked at her for several seconds, never pausing in what he was doing. She thought for sure he was going to send her away, which would be stupid. Finally she saw acquiescence in his eyes.

"Plastic cup," he said, pointing to a stack. "Just about everything goes in a plastic cup here." She grabbed three plastic cups. "Start with vodka." He set a shot glass in front of her. "Fill that for each drink."

She did as he said and noticed he was still working on his own cocktails.

"Add tomato juice." He pointed at the recessed cooler.

She was clumsy and afraid of making a bigger mess than they already had. Carefully, she poured in the juice. Derek finished what he was doing and watched her slow progress for a few excruciating seconds. He handed his drinks to her.

"Guy in the bright blue shirt by the register. Already paid."

She delivered them, and when she returned to Derek, he was adding a shrimp garnish on her Bloody Marys. She took them without a word and placed them in front of the customer, then went to the kitchen, hoping Miss Friendly had some shrimp for her. There were two cardboard containers of shrimp and cocktail sauce on the counter next to the doorway. Macey hesitated half a second, then grabbed them.

The next hour and a half flew by, the only conversation between her and Derek being directions for mixing drinks. How did these people imbibe this early in the day, anyway? It wasn't even one o'clock yet.

The crowd finally thinned, everyone served for the moment, and Macey took a deep breath. Sweat curled the hair at her temples and ran between her breasts. She copied Derek and picked up a towel to start scrubbing all the surfaces.

"Place looks like a bomb went off," said a gravelly voiced old man who had just taken the third stool over. He wore a light blue bucket hat over his wispy white hair, and a wild floral button-down shirt.

"You're late," Derek said to the guy.

"I'm not on the clock anymore, so I guess that doesn't matter much."

Macey's confusion must've shown on her face because when Derek glanced at her, he explained. "My uncle. Gus. Former owner."

Apparently the introduction ended there. Macey held out her hand. "Nice to meet you, Derek's uncle Gus. I'm Derek's friend Macey."

Gus took her hand and held it longer than necessary, but not in a dirty-old-man way. He smiled and his eyes crinkled at the corners, as if he'd laughed a lot in his lifetime. "Pleased to meet you, Macey. Didn't realize he had any friends."

"Met him when I was five and didn't know any better."

Gus howled and nodded in appreciation as Derek set a drink in front of him.

"This straight?" Gus asked Derek.

"Pure whiskey."

"I can taste if you watered it down."

"That's why I don't. But you only get one."

"We'll see," Gus said, and took a swallow. He grunted in self-righteous approval.

"We have this argument every single day," Derek said to Macey as he went back to cleaning the counter.

"Boy tries to mother me," Gus said. "It's okay for a pretty lady to mother me but he's not so pretty."

No, *pretty* wasn't a word she'd use to describe Derek. Sexy as all get-out, maybe. And the fact that he tried to keep this gruff old man in line was endearing, especially as grumpy as Derek had been to her.

"That's why you like it at the old folks' home," Derek said. "All those nurses waiting on you hand and foot. They'd have my hide if I put you on the bus tanked."

Macey turned to the work area along the back wall and started putting lids on the containers of fruit slices in the cooler. The limes were gone and the lemons were low. "Do you have more fruit?"

"You don't have to help," Derek said as he organized the liquor bottles on the shelves above.

"You need help." In more ways than one, but she wasn't foolish enough to mention it. "Are you planning to hire someone?"

"I'm working on it."

"Do you have any applicants?"

"I said I'm working on it."

"I told him a month ago he needed to hire people," Gus said.

The unsmiling girl from the back room appeared and filled her glass with ice and lemonade, watching Macey. "He doesn't take suggestions well."

"He never has," Macey said, sensing that this other female might be an ally in spite of her chilly demeanor.

The girl had a rough edge to her. She wore a black, body-hugging tee, old, torn jeans and heavy combat boots. Her shiny dark hair looked baby soft, an interesting contrast to her otherwise hard facade. "He works open to close, seven days a week. Tell me that's not insane."

"I'm right here," Derek snarled. "I can hear every word you say."

"But you don't *listen,*" the girl said.

"I'll second that," Gus muttered from the counter.

"I'm Macey. I grew up with the stubborn one."

"Andie. You're familiar with his hardheadedness then."

"Very. Open to close...how many hours is that?" Macey asked.

"From 10:00 a.m. to 2:00 a.m. You do the math."

The math said he was about two steps away from exhaustion.

"No wonder you look so tired," Macey said to Derek. "You can't do that."

"I'm used to twenty-four-hour shifts."

"But at the fire department, you got several days off in a row."

"Andie, could you show her where the limes are in back?"

Andie stared at him as she sipped her drink. "Firefighter? I've worked with you for four weeks and you've never said a word."

"I've said as much about my past as you've said about yours," Derek pointed out.

"Mine isn't interesting. What's a firefighter doing in a place like this?"

"Tending bar."

"You must be hiding from someone," Andie speculated, her head tilting as she sized him up.

Or some*thing*, Macey thought to herself. That Derek hadn't told Andie about what was such a basic part of him concerned her more than anything else. Firefighting had been more than just his job, it'd been his life. And it appeared he'd given it up completely.

DEREK HAD MADE ANDIE go home at midnight, when they'd finally closed the grill. He'd tried to get Macey to leave then, too, but she'd refused. Then a large group of customers descended on them and he didn't have time to argue. At one point, as they'd both prepared drinks, she'd shot him a smug look, as if to say he wouldn't have been able to handle the crush of business if she'd left. That made him irritable, possibly because she might've been right.

All he wanted to do was close the bar, go home and collapse. He'd screwed up big-time not hiring someone before now. Gus had warned him, but Derek had had no concept of how many people would suddenly infiltrate the island as soon as schools were out for the summer all over the state of Texas. He felt as if he could sleep for a week, except, of course, he wouldn't sleep much at all once he turned in.

They'd just served last call and had started cleaning. A couple of small groups still hung around the high U-shaped counter skirting the perimeter of the shack, and closing time was only ten minutes away.

"Hey," Macey said, clearly nervous for some reason. "I meant to ask you earlier...would you mind if I stayed at your place while I'm here?"

He'd been mopping up spills on the counter with a towel that was too wet, but froze at her question. A houseguest appealed to him about as much as having someone take a baseball bat to his head. He'd let her stay there last night only because she'd been sound asleep when he found her. He didn't want anyone witnessing his nightly living room–TV pattern or anything else about his screwed-up life. Especially someone who would report back to his mom. He was surprised she hadn't trooped down here herself.

"I don't know, Mace...."

She quickly shook her head, disappointment in her eyes. "Forget I said anything. I can find a hotel."

He put the towel down. "Look, I know my mom sent you. I'm okay. I don't need anyone spying on me."

"Spying? I wasn't going to spy."

"But my mom did send you. Didn't she?" There was no question in his mind; he just wanted Macey to admit it.

"Actually, she advised me not to come. Mentioned you were difficult to be around."

That summarized it well. "I came to the island to be alone. No offense, Macey, but I need some space. From everyone."

"I understand."

But he could tell she didn't. No one did, and he didn't expect them to. As long as they left him alone.

"I'm not good company. You're better off staying somewhere else."

"Yeah. I get it." She finished putting everything in its place. "Okay if I head out?"

"Of course." Considering he'd tried to get her to go hours before. Multiple times. Not to mention she wasn't an official employee. "Come by tomorrow and I'll pay you for the day."

She nodded absently and got her orange soda from under the counter before leaving.

"Macey," he said, knowing what a complete asshole he was being not to let her stay with him.

She looked back over her shoulder.

"Thanks for helping today."

The smile she sent his way was forced, nothing like the genuine one she'd had for customers all day. But he supposed it was better than the response he deserved.

This was exactly why he'd told her no. As mean as it was for him to turn her away, his transgressions would stack up higher if he agreed to let her stick around. While he didn't like to hurt her, he was just doing what he had to do.

CHAPTER THREE

MACEY HAD NEVER BEEN much of a door slammer. But when she got to her car, still outside of Derek's condo, a ways up the beach from the bar, she swung the door shut so hard she was surprised it didn't fall off the hinges.

She leaned over the steering wheel, exhausted. She hadn't helped Derek out all day in the bar so that he'd feel obligated to let her stay with him. But the fact she could do that for him and then he wouldn't let her sleep on his couch...

She pounded the steering wheel and started the ignition. Pulling onto the street, she had no idea where she was going. All she knew was she needed a bed, preferably ten minutes ago.

The island apparently had two main streets—one on the bay side and this one, on the gulf side. Hotels, condos, souvenir shops, bars and restaurants lined both, and houses—some of them built on stilts in case of flooding—lined the perpendicular streets in between. She'd stop at the first hotel she came to that didn't look as if it would cost her a fortune, and get a room for one night. Tomorrow she'd search for a longer-term rental. Derek might think he could scare her off, but he was wrong with a capital *W*. He'd ticked her off enough tonight that she'd stay around to bother him just out of obstinacy.

Thirty minutes later, Macey struggled to come up with plan B. There were no vacancies. Not even at the seedy hotels. According to the night manager at the last one, she'd be lucky to find anything tonight.

Her options were limited—okay, almost nonexistent. She could keep trying hotels, hoping that one of them had a spare broom closet to rent out before she keeled over, or she could find a place to park and succumb to sleep.

She drove up to the next chain hotel and turned into the driveway. Scanning the parking lot, she couldn't see an empty space anywhere. As she pulled into the check-in lane outside the main door, she peered inside. Might as well give this one last place a try. If they didn't have something, she'd sleep in the car.

She had her answer within thirty seconds. Toyota Inn it was. She fell into the seat and started the engine. Without knowing where she was heading, she went back the way she'd come, driving slowly, looking for a place to park where she wouldn't be bothered, wouldn't have a bright light in her face and hopefully wouldn't have the police called in.

She was back to Derek's bar before she realized it, and almost didn't recognize it all sealed up tight for the night. Closed and dark. And owned by someone she knew wouldn't call the cops. She turned in and pulled up as close as she could get to the building.

Her eyes watered from fatigue as she turned off the

ignition. She popped the trunk from inside, then climbed out to open her suitcase. She dug through it until she found her University of Texas sweatshirt, and pulled it over her head. She didn't even bother to reclose the suitcase, just shut the trunk and went back to the driver's side and sank in. She reclined the seat all the way back, curled up on her side and passed out almost immediately, not allowing herself a single thought about Derek.

IT WASN'T THE HILTON, but the driver's seat wasn't much worse than the thin mattresses Macey had slept on for two years in Thailand. She opened her eyes and checked her watch. Twenty after eight. The morning sun was beating down on the car and she was covered with sweat. To sleep through the growing heat and all the people out and about... She frowned when she raised the seat and realized how public her metal campsite was.

She glanced around to make sure she didn't have an audience, and wondered how many beachgoers had ambled close enough to the car to notice her sleeping. She should be embarrassed, but she hadn't had many alternatives at two-thirty in the morning.

After grabbing a change of clothes from her suitcase, Macey hurried to the public restroom outside Derek's bar. She'd shower as soon as she had a private bathroom.

That was her first order of business this morning—finding a place to rent for the next five or six weeks. Actually, make that the second priority. Her stomach rumbled so loudly she was afraid others would hear it.

She drove to the grocery store she'd spotted on her

way into town. Minutes later she took a maple-frosted doughnut, a bottle of grape juice and a vacation rental magazine out onto the beach, down a ways from Derek's bar and in the opposite direction from his condo. She wasn't ready to see him yet. Would have to prepare herself mentally—and physically, for that matter. It was going to take some effort to act as if everything was fine and he hadn't hurt her.

HER NEW APARTMENT had seen better days. Probably about thirty years ago. But when the sixtyish property-management lady had mentioned that two "hunky" firefighters lived in the same building, Macey hadn't been able to resist the place. It wasn't the "hunk" factor that attracted her, though if the woman was right in her assessment that would make things all the more interesting. Macey was plotting, hoping to find out more about the local department, with the ultimate goal of somehow getting Derek to recognize that's where he belonged. Time off from firefighting, she understood. But she was afraid he might never let himself return, and that would be a shame.

So now, in addition to firefighting neighbors, she had a shower that stayed hot for a good eight and a half minutes, a tiny kitchen with appliances from an avocado-green era, and a bed—luxuriously queen-size, no less.

Best of all, she had a minuscule view. Her budget didn't come anywhere close to covering an apartment directly on the beach, so she'd have to settle for a bedroom window a block and a half from the gulf. While the view was partially blocked by condos, she could see actual blue water. And sand and sky. There was a desk in front of the window, which would make a perfect place for her to work.

She'd already unpacked her outdated pre–Peace Corps laptop and set it up on the desk, and couldn't wait to dive in. The Peace Corps Web site and literature had promised a life-changing experience, and that's exactly what Macey had gotten. Not only had it altered her personally, given her more confidence, a broader view of the world and more appreciation for the advantages of growing up in the U.S., but it had changed her career goals significantly.

Prior to Asia, she'd hoped to use her business degree to go into project management with a large firm somewhere. Her job in Thailand had been to help villagers and rural residents set up their own businesses to provide for their families. Compared to her corporate dreams, she'd been working on a minute scale—with farmers, fishermen, weavers and so many other services that Americans gave little thought to. She'd loved it. The change those people had been able to make in their lives with her assistance in business planning had humbled her, lit a spark deep inside of her.

Now she wanted to do something similar in Dallas, her hometown, specifically assisting single women. She intended to use her so-called vacation on the island to develop her nonprofit foundation's own business plan. She wanted to start it up before the end of the year.

Macey finished unpacking her clothes and putting

them into the beat-up dresser in the furnished apartment. She checked her watch to make sure it was late enough for her next objective of the day: lobbying Derek for a job.

It was twelve forty-five. Perfect. She had just enough time to get dressed and head over there. And if a little manipulation had to come into play to get her way, so be it.

"HIRE ME," Macey said from the customer side of the bar just after the insanity called lunch died down.

Derek stared at her as he helped himself to a Coke. "Thought you were on vacation."

"I need the cash."

Stalling as he tried to come up with a good objection, he took a drink and checked that the fan pointing behind the bar was on high. "You don't know a Tom Collins from an Adam and Eve."

"I can learn."

"I'll teach her," Gus said from right next to her.

"Why am I not surprised you're on her side?" he asked his uncle.

Andie came in from the back room then, on her way out. She normally worked a split shift, helping over lunch and returning at dinner each evening until the grill closed. Except for yesterday... There'd been no split in her shift because business had never slowed down enough. Because, yeah...he needed more people.

"I'm leaving," she said, then spotted Macey. "Hey, what were you doing sleeping in your car this morning?"

Macey's cheeks turned pink and she stared at the plastic cup in front of her. "Um, sleeping. Everything was full last night."

"And Super Derek didn't take you in? Nice." Andie shot a scowl his way and shook her head as she walked out of the bar.

Derek wanted to hit something. He was such a bastard. But what the hell was he supposed to do? The effort it took for him to be nice was more than he could handle.

"Mixed drinks are a foreign concept to you," he said to Macey, refusing to acknowledge the whole sleeping-in-the-car conversation. "Your idea of a good drink is a wine cooler."

"Which you sadly don't even have, so I guess there's no chance of me getting drunk on the clock."

"She needs the exposure to more appealing cocktails, Derek, you've got to admit," Gus said matter-of-factly. "You'd be doing her a service."

She was trying to worm her way into his life, dammit. He knew this and he hated it, but he hated the thought of trying to find reliable employees more. The island had been full of flakes before high season, and he'd bet the whole bar and everything in it there'd be even more infiltrating the area now.

Besides, hiring her would be a peace offering after last night. He leaned against the back counter, which still needed cleaning.

He'd promised Gus to return The Shell Shack to being *the* place to hang out on the island, as it was before Gus had had to close down last year. If word got out the service sucked or there was a thirty-minute wait for a beer, that wouldn't happen. Macey could help him turn things around. She was the business queen, after all.

"Fine," he said. "Five bucks an hour until you have half a clue what you're doing."

"So start teaching me some drinks," she said easily, and he felt like the worst kind of jerk. She was only trying to help him.

"Eat something first." He motioned to the kitchen in back. "Fast, before the next bunch of people shows up."

"Yes, sir." Macey saluted him. "You should eat, too."

"No, and don't think just because I gave you a job that you can butt in to my life or make me eat."

"Whatever you say, Dare."

He could tell by the look on her face that she didn't mean a word of it. There was no question in his mind he would live to regret his latest hire.

CHAPTER FOUR

"YOU'RE WALKING HOME?" Derek asked as he locked the last set of shutters on the bar that night.

"Yes, I'm walking home. I happen to love walking on the beach."

"Where's home?"

Macey refused to let a smart-aleck retort about since-when-did-he-care slip out. The less he knew about how much he'd upset her last night, the better. "Home is that way," she said, pointing vaguely.

"Not your car?"

"Not my car. One night of that is plenty, thanks." *Oops*. She couldn't help herself.

"Macey, I'm really sorry about—"

She held up her hand. "It's fine, Dare." She grabbed her purse and the orange soda she'd just refilled. "See you tomorrow. Want me here at ten?"

"Noon's fine. Business doesn't pick up till then. Macey, wait," he said as she started down the concrete steps from the sprawling patio dotted with weatherproof metal tables and chairs.

She turned toward him and waited as he locked the door and checked it.

"I'll drive you home."

"I want to walk."

"You didn't used to be this stubborn."

"It's less than a mile. I'll be fine."

He stared at her under the bright light that illuminated the patio and the hotel next door. "I'm walking you home, then."

"You were *always* this stubborn." Macey was actually glad to see any hint of the Derek she used to know, and couldn't hold back a smile. "Suit yourself."

She started walking and Derek caught up without hesitation.

"You do know I've spent the past two years on my own in a foreign country?" she said as they padded through the cushiony, dry sand.

He didn't respond. *Fantastic.* She had herself a silent, brooding chaperone. Ignoring his moodiness, she took in the beauty around her. The thundering waves rolled in, fascinating her. Frightening her at the same time they lulled her. Kind of like Derek.

She angled toward the water, but stopped just short of it. Her aching feet cried out for it, but the salt would sting the cut on her foot, regardless of the thick bandages she'd layered on.

"So what's Andie's story?" she asked, wanting to get Derek to talk. About anything.

"No idea."

"You hired her. You've got to know something about her."

"I know her last name, that she rides a motorcycle and that she shows up for work when she's supposed to."

"Is she a local?" Macey tried not to cringe at the very large gap in his info.

"Don't think so. She travels."

"Travels." Derek wasn't normally an idiot, but hiring someone without getting basic information, references… That was something Macey would never do.

"She's worked out," he said defensively.

"So far."

"Andie's fine. I trust her."

"Yeah," Macey said, realizing she did, too, strangely enough. "But I'll handle the hiring from now on if you don't mind."

"Be my guest." His tone was indifferent, not at all offended.

"Gorgeous night," she said, stooping to pick up a shell that gleamed in the moonlight.

The air was still warm, and thick with moisture. Stars peppered the cloudless sky and the sliver of a moon hung delicately over the gulf. There were couples and small groups of people scattered here and there along the beach, but no one close.

This place spoke to something deep inside her. She was drawn to the water as if she'd lived her whole life here, as if it were a part of her she'd been missing. She filled her lungs with the salty air, and a calm settled over her.

They made their way along the shore in silence. Derek stared straight ahead, she noticed, as if he was oblivious to the serenity, the beauty. But then Derek had always been Mr. Practical.

"You should check out the scenery sometime," she said, smiling. "*This* is why I choose to walk."

He looked at her as if he'd forgotten she was there. "Huh?"

Macey swept her hand out to indicate, well, everything. How anyone could be numb to these surroundings she didn't know. But then again, she couldn't begin to imagine what dark ugly place Derek was stuck in.

"So the bar made lots of money today," she said in an attempt to keep the topic neutral. "We almost managed to keep up with the customers."

"Yeah."

"I thought I'd post Help Wanted fliers around town," she continued. "I figure we need at least four more people, maybe more if they only want part-time work."

"Okay."

"And maybe once we hire them, we could rent them out as escorts after hours."

"Sure. Wait…what?"

"Just making certain you're paying attention. The escort business would get us some bad press, huh?"

Derek finally looked at her—really looked at her. She tried to hide her grin.

"Kidding," she said, focusing on the shell-speckled sand. "That was a joke."

"Interesting idea. But likely to give Gus a heart attack."

"He's something else, isn't he?" She chuckled, thinking about the cantankerous act Derek's uncle put on to, she suspected, get a reaction from Derek.

"He means well. He just insists on being annoying about it."

"I like him."

"That's right—you two are best friends. How much farther to your place?"

"You don't have to walk me all the way home. I'm perfectly safe."

Derek glanced around. "All kinds of yo-yos out here."

She loved his protective tendency, even if it was just the way he was with everyone. She used to dream that it meant something special between them, but she'd long ago resigned herself to the reality that it didn't. She'd forced herself to move on.

Mostly.

When she sneaked a sideways glance at his profile, she shivered. In the dim moonlight, the weary shadows on his face were invisible and only the strong angles stood out. He looked like the Derek she'd grown up with instead of the one carrying the weight of tragedy on his shoulders.

"My path is past that next hotel," she told him, gesturing toward the Casa del Mar. "I can make it from here."

"Maybe I want to see where you're staying."

"Did I mention how stubborn you are?"

"A time or two today so far."

"Is this guilt-induced? Is that why you insist on seeing me home?"

"If it is, go with it. My kind, unselfish gestures are at a premium."

As if she hadn't noticed.

A few minutes later, Derek climbed the flight of stairs with her to her second-floor apartment.

"There's really not much to see yet," she told him. "Generic furniture that came with the place is all. Not even any pet dust bunnies."

She unlocked the door and pushed it open.

"You should put a dead bolt on this," Derek said, following her in.

"Says the man who leaves his door unlocked for anyone to come in off the streets."

"Lucky for you."

"Want a snack?" she asked, heading into the bathroom-size kitchenette. "I'm starving. I've got Cheez-Its, trail mix and Ding Dongs."

"On a health kick?"

"On the rebound from very little junk food for two years. Nearly killed me."

She took out the box of Ding Dongs and grabbed two packages of chocolaty heaven. She held one out for him but he gravely shook his head.

"You're saying no to Ding Dongs?" She ripped hers open and took a big bite, closing her eyes to savor the sweetness. "Your loss."

There was a day when Derek would've razzed her for a good ten minutes over her nutritionally lacking cuisine, but now he stared at the half-eaten cake as if it'd be the death of her. She watched him as she chewed, missing that easy smile that was once such a big part of him. "Sit," she said, motioning to the floor in front of the functional, boxy sofa.

"I need to get home."

"Why? So you can fall asleep watching TV?" she asked on a hunch. The look on his face confirmed he hadn't just slept in his chair the other night because she'd invaded his bed. She'd bet money he crashed on the chair regularly.

Derek sat heavily on the sofa.

"Not there," Macey said. "Floor."

"You want me to sit on the floor."

"Trust me for once."

He looked at her warily as she finished off the second Ding Dong and licked the filling off her fingers.

"You just ate two of those things in thirty seconds flat."

"Yes."

"And you want me to trust you."

She nodded and washed her hands in the kitchen sink. "Down," she said as she approached the sofa.

He lowered himself to the floor with a stoic expression. Macey climbed onto the sofa directly behind him and started rubbing his shoulders. His muscles were so tight he actually flinched when she applied pressure.

"Wow," Macey said. "You're one giant knot."

"Probably from being forced to sleep on the chair by some wayward chick who stole my bed."

"Right." Macey worked her thumbs near his spine.

"This mess isn't the kind that happens overnight. Relax."

"I *am* relaxing."

She flicked him in the side of the head. "If this is relaxing then I'm the quarterback for the Cowboys."

"It's as good as it gets."

And that's why he needed her. If he was this twisted up on the outside, she hated to imagine what he was like on the inside.

"Lie down," she said, getting off the sofa.

Derek looked up at her with something between temptation and annoyance. "You've gotten bossy."

"I've always been bossy. I just used to hide it well." Macey patted the cushion. "You know you want to."

"No. I don't."

"Why not? Your neck is a mess and I'd wager money your back is just as bad."

"It's late."

"The sooner you lie down, the sooner you can go home and sleep on your chair."

Derek stood with an aggravated grunt. "I won't fit on that couch."

She looked at the sofa and looked at him. "You're right. You'll have to settle for the floor." No way could she let him stretch out on her bed. A big, muscled firefighter in her bed would be a very dangerous thing.

He studied her. "You're not going to let this go, are you?"

Maybe it was stupid of her to push him but this was something she could do. She couldn't take away his grief or his pain or any of the other hard-core emotions he was wrestling—or avoiding wrestling—but she could help him physically relax.

Macey stared him down and pointed at the floor.

"You couldn't follow my mom's advice," he muttered as he kicked his shoes off and pulled his shirt over his head. Macey sucked in her breath at the sight of his naked chest. She really needed to be careful what she wished for. Admiring him while he slept was one thing, but touching him? With no shirt? In a different lifetime it would be her own personal nirvana, but now? Torture.

Tough job but somebody had to do it.

He lay on his stomach on the beige carpet that looked almost new. He rested his head on his arms, giving her a fantastic view of biceps, triceps and what have you. In addition to the Longhorn on his arm, he had a tattoo of a firefighter's cross on the upper left side of his back.

Macey settled on the floor next to him and started working the shoulder blade closest to her, digging into the cords of muscle. As she'd guessed, they were strung tight.

"You need a professional," she told him as she ran her thumb back and forth over a stubborn knot.

"Does that mean I can go home?"

"Not until you admit this feels good."

His response was a noncommittal sound in his throat.

After several minutes of deep tissue massage on one shoulder, Macey switched to his right side and started in. "This side's even worse."

Derek didn't say anything, didn't stir, and she wondered if he'd gone to sleep. Could he have relaxed that much? When she finished, she glanced at his face, and saw his eyes remained closed. She stood quietly, staring down at this beautiful male specimen, trying not to think too hard about how amazing it was to touch him, to feel the strength of him on such a personal level.

To best reach the rest of his back, she tentatively straddled his hips and lowered herself to sit on his butt. His tight, perfect butt.

Forget trying to keep this clinical. She was only human.

She ran her hands over his skin along the waistband of his shorts, from his sides to his spine. She feasted her eyes on the ridges of muscle that disappeared beneath the garment, imagining what he must look like out of it. Digging her fingers into those ridges, she elicited a low groan from him. The sound was erotic, or maybe her mind was just in the wrong place.

"Pressure okay?" she asked in a half whisper.

"More than."

She couldn't help but wonder what it would be like to make love to this man. What would it be like to touch him wherever she wanted, to have him touch her? To have him *want* her?

Her breath hitched, snapping her to attention. She sincerely hoped he hadn't heard that.

She sucked in oxygen until her lungs were full, and let it out slowly, quietly.

"Tell me about the fire," she said softly.

Just like that, he tensed. She could see and feel the change even though he was facedown. She figured she'd just screwed up a good half hour of work. But she refused to take back the question.

"Dare?"

It took an eternity for him to say anything. "Not going there."

"Why?"

Okay, not the brightest question, but that's what popped out. Anything to get him to say more. She hated this helpless feeling, her inability to do him any good.

He rolled to his side and started to get up, sending her to the floor. "It's time for me to go."

"Derek, wait. I'm sorry." She put her hand on his shoulder. "No more questions. Just let me finish your massage. I'll see if I can undo the damage I just caused."

He studied her unhappily.

"Or are you afraid you'll end up admitting how good it feels?" The corners of her lips betrayed a half smile.

Her challenge had the desired effect. After he narrowed his eyes, he lay down on his stomach again.

"How 'bout those Astros?"

Derek gave what could almost be considered a chuckle. "Smart girl."

"That's the nicest thing you've said to me since I've been here." She tried to make her tone light. "So what's up with Gus? What's his story?"

"He's my dad's brother. He and another guy opened The Shell Shack fifteen years ago."

"What happened to the other guy?"

"He followed a woman to the West Coast. Handed his half over."

"And now the whole thing's yours."

She went to work on his upper arms, not allowing herself to consider how hard they were, how sculpted.

"God, that feels good."

She smiled to herself in victory. It was all she could do not to say she'd told him so.

After several minutes of silence, Derek said, "When I came here, I agreed to help Gus."

"Help him?"

"He had to close the bar down when he moved into assisted living. It was killing him to watch it sit there and rot."

"So you agreed to reopen it."

"I shouldn't have. It'll be worse for Gus when I run it into the damn ground."

She stopped massaging. "You're not going to run it into the ground."

Derek rolled over and sat up. He reached for his shirt and put it back on. She actually saw him shutter his expression. "I need to get home, let you sleep."

It was after three and she couldn't hold back a yawn as she stood. "*You* need to get some sleep, now that your muscles are untied."

He stood up in turn and nodded. "I owe you one, Mace."

"Maybe I'll hold you to that."

As she saw him out, she did her best to fight off the images of the ways he could make it up to her. What a lousy friend she was if she couldn't keep her mind off her own pointless desires long enough to just be there for him. She'd have to do a lot better at keeping her thoughts under control than she'd done tonight.

CHAPTER FIVE

MACEY WAS IN SERIOUS NEED of a nap, and that was saying something for a girl who didn't take naps, not even when she was a baby, if her mother's tales of woe were true.

Bar hours were going to be an adjustment. Normally she was in bed by ten and got up with the birds. Today, she'd stupidly still gotten up with the birds, even though she'd slept for only a few brief hours. Add to the equation the restless R-rated dreams featuring Derek, and she felt as if she could sleep for a week straight.

She had two hours before work, so here she was, standing in front of the mirror on the back of her bedroom door, trying to get up the nerve to walk out to the apartment complex's pool in her new swimsuit. It was a steal—$15.99 at one of the stores screaming out to tourists with five-dollar T-shirts advertised in the windows.

She didn't normally do bikinis. In fact, she'd started with one-piece suits in the store, but a very persuasive, good-looking male employee had acted as if she was about to commit a major sin. He'd steered her to the two-pieces. A bright orange-and-yellow suit with gold metallic designs on it had caught her eye, and since it was five bucks cheaper than the one-piece suits, she'd somehow been suckered in.

And now here she stood. Unused to having so much skin showing. The sales guy had said it was a modest suit, but he wasn't the one who had to wear it.

Shaking her head, she tied her new beach towel around her waist and went to the door. On her way out, she picked up a can of pop, her new novel and a bottle of SPF 50 sunscreen. Red wasn't her best color.

The second she stepped outside, she knew. The two men dripping testosterone in the deep end of the pool were the firefighters she'd been hoping to meet. Turned out the property-management woman had understated the situation. These guys weren't "hunky." That was like saying today's 102° temperature was "warmish."

There were a handful of other people enjoying the pool and deck, but it'd be impossible to miss the two firemen even if there'd been a huge crowd. Both had classic all-American good looks—they could almost be brothers with their short dark hair, suntanned faces and legions of muscles—and that was just what she could discern above the water's surface. Vibrant energy seemed to surround them.

Macey had to will herself to turn her attention away. She scouted the deck for an available lounge chair, spotting one to the left, at the far end of the pool. As she walked toward it, she could feel their eyes on her. She reminded herself the guy at the store had sworn the bikini looked "delicious" on her and that she was tired of being the plain girl, but she tingled with self-consciousness.

Keeping her eyes forward, which took some effort, she sat sideways on the lounger and unloaded her things, stalling, trying to summon her courage. Approaching guys like them wasn't her usual MO but it'd be worth it to know someone in the local fire department. Such a hardship, she thought to herself, and stifled a grin.

By the time she stood, their attention was elsewhere and they'd moved to the shallow end, which gave Macey the opportunity to inconspicuously sit on the near side of the pool and dangle her feet in the water.

Suddenly the guys were both speeding toward her end in what appeared to be an all-out freestyle race. They touched the wall, one on each side of her.

"I won," the one on her right said as he surfaced noisily.

"About time. I was starting to feel sorry for you." The man on her left lifted himself effortlessly out of the pool and sat a couple of feet away from Macey. "Hello."

"Hi," she said, deciding he was the type who likely got any girl he wanted. Besides the extreme self-confidence that spilled over into cockiness, and the already noted biceps, he had startlingly blue eyes and a smile full of confidence-inspiring charm.

"He didn't beat me by more than an inch, did he?" he asked.

"Evan, let her be. I'm sure she has better things to do than massage your bruised elephant-size ego." The guy on her right remained in the water. His hair was a few shades darker, almost black, and he had dreamy choco-late eyes and a square chin. His manner was plenty tinged with testosterone, but she determined instantly that he was more laid-back than his friend.

"Evan Drake," the one sitting next to her said, holding out a wet hand. "That's Clay Marlow. You must be the new neighbor."

She shook his hand. "I'm Macey. Which apartment is yours?"

"Opposite end of the second floor from you."

"How'd you know which one's mine?"

"He has a built-in single-woman radar," Clay said. "You'll have to forgive him for being so obvious."

"I just pay attention," Evan said. The smile he gave her was openly flirtatious but it didn't have the desired effect on Macey. Her type, if she had one, leaned toward more down-to-earth. His forwardness scared her off. She assumed, whether rightly or wrongly, he was only interested in one thing, and that wasn't Macey's scene at all.

"Are you new to the island?" Evan asked.

"Just visiting, actually. For a few weeks. What about you two?"

"Permanent residents."

"Beach bums?" she asked, smiling, knowing full well they weren't.

"We work for the fire department."

Just the opening she was looking for.

"A good friend of mine was a firefighter in Dallas. Now he runs a bar here."

"Dallas, huh? Cool. Does he want to get back into it?"

"Maybe someday. He's pretty busy right now. Is the

station nearby?" She'd heard sirens a couple of times during the night, but hadn't been able to tell where they'd originated.

Evan nodded. "On the beach about half a mile south." He pointed in that direction. "We like this place because it's close and cheap."

"And furnished, too," Macey said. "Plus the minuscule view of the ocean."

"Our view is the pool, which seems to suit his purposes," Clay said, gesturing toward Evan.

"You make it sound like keeping track of the local females is a sin," Evan complained.

"More like an art, in your case."

"Just a pastime."

"Everyone needs a hobby," Macey said, surprised to find she was enjoying herself with these two.

"What's yours?" Evan asked, and she found herself momentarily stumped.

"Good question. I need to find one. I've been in Thailand for two years and didn't have the opportunity for hobbies."

"Thailand?" Evan asked.

Macey nodded. "Peace Corps."

"Whoa. Never would've guessed," he said. Macey tried not to take the comment personally. She couldn't help it, though. She looked plain and boring and not at all like the type who would take off on an adventure on the other side of the world.

"What are you doing on such a long vacation?" Clay

asked as he treaded water several feet in front of her and Evan.

"Recuperating from the Peace Corps and starting a nonprofit organization."

"Is that all?" Evan asked with a sexy grin that would win over ninety percent of the female population in a nanosecond.

Macey realized suddenly that she had no idea how long she'd been talking. She hopped up and walked over to her belongings and checked the time. "Actually, no. I'm also helping my friend out at his bar. The Shell Shack. I need to go shower if I'm going to be on time."

"Pleasure to meet you, Macey," Evan said, standing.

Clay nodded politely, and she waved as she hurried from the pool deck to her apartment. Part one of her mission accomplished: she had some friends in the local fire department. That, undoubtedly, was the easy part.

DEREK DID A DOUBLE TAKE when Macey stepped behind the counter at two minutes till noon. She was dressed unlike he'd ever seen her before, wearing short white shorts and a body-hugging blue tee. She had curves he'd never noticed, likely because she'd never shown them off. Surely he'd notice *that*, wouldn't he?

Jeez, a good night's sleep must be messing with his mind. This was *Macey*. That she was solely responsible for the best six hours of sleep he'd had in months didn't escape him. Hell, maybe he should hire her to rub his aching muscles every night and tuck him in instead of pouring drinks and wiping down counters all day.

"Sorry I'm late," she said, barely looking at him as she grabbed a cup and filled it with orange soda.

"You're two minutes early."

"That's late."

Derek shook his head and proceeded to take an order from the couple who'd just come in.

The next hour and a half sped by. The three of them—Macey, he and Andie, in back—were developing a good rhythm, although Macey still had to ask what went into a drink every few minutes. He knew she'd learn. Macey was smart and caught on fast. His hesitation in hiring her had nothing to do with her competence. When they'd been in high school waiting tables at Grace's, he'd always looked forward to sharing shifts with her because she pulled her weight without fail.

The lunch rush eventually died down to a steady flow. Macey joined him at the back work area as he mixed a vodka sour.

"There's a guy I want to interview for a position waiting for me outside. I'm going to see how far I can get before you're buried again."

"Someone to hire?" he asked, looking beyond her, trying to spot the individual.

"Hopefully. The past hour's been insane."

Insane, possibly. A way to pass the time without a chance to think about things you didn't want to think about, definitely.

"Macey's been here two days and already doing what you couldn't manage in two months."

Derek didn't flinch at the gravelly voice. He grabbed a cup and poured whiskey, then served it to Gus.

"This straight?" the old man asked.

"You know it is. I tried to dilute it once," he said to Macey. She smiled as she headed out to do the interview.

"You learned your lesson, didn't you?" Gus said smugly.

"Isn't there a nurse somewhere who wants to coddle and nurture your obstinate ass?"

"They all do. I needed a break."

Derek cracked a smile. "Want anything to eat?"

"Some chips is all. Had a steak for lunch."

"Remind me to move in with you when I get a chance." He grabbed a bag of salt-and-vinegar chips—Gus's favorite—and tossed it on the counter in front of him.

"They wouldn't take you even if it wasn't just for old farts."

"They'd see I have the same last name as you and lock the doors, I reckon."

"So the amazing Macey is going to save your butt, it appears." Gus took a good-size swig.

"It appears." Derek kept his tone bored, unwilling to show his relief.

He'd never had a head for business. Never needed to. In school, he'd studied exercise science and avoided anything business related. The thought of budgets and suits and ties had always made his eyes glaze over, and when he'd agreed to take the bar from Gus, he hadn't been in his right mind. Hadn't thought about much beyond pouring a drink here and there.

Andie came out of the back room, crunching on a tortilla chip.

"You want to go home for a couple hours?" Derek asked.

"Doesn't matter to me. If you can pay me for working straight through, I'm game."

"I can pay you. Do you do anything besides work and sleep?"

"You should talk."

"Do you?"

"Since when are you concerned about what I do when I leave here?" Her tone was light, but he sensed she wasn't going to answer his question straight. Andie had been tight-lipped when he'd hired her, explaining only that she didn't stay anywhere for long, but that she'd be a reliable employee while she was here. Maybe not his first choice in people to hire, but back in April, there hadn't been anyone else falling into his lap, so to speak, and he hadn't been able to face hunting for employees, regardless of Gus's nagging.

"Just trying to be friendly," Derek said.

"I didn't recognize it. You snarl so much better."

Gus cackled from his chair, reminding Derek he was there and had pretty good hearing for an old dude.

"I could fire you, you know," Derek told Andie. "I have another employee now. Maybe even two if Macey works her magic."

Andie grinned. "Fire away, baby."

"Nah. No one flips burgers quite like you do."

"Keeping this one in line will take both you girls," Gus interjected.

Andie acknowledged Gus's comment with a nod and returned to the back room just as another group of people stepped up to the counter. She preferred to work behind the scenes whenever there was a choice, though she could serve drinks just fine.

Derek was still taking orders and making drinks when Macey returned a few minutes later. She set some papers in the kitchen, under her purse. Derek watched the guy she'd been talking to walk off, and wondered if he was old enough to work in a bar.

"Well?" Derek said, delivering the last of an order as she came back into the bar area.

"Done deal. Starts tomorrow."

"Has he hit puberty yet?"

"He's twenty-three. Needs money."

"Shouldn't I have met him before you hired him?"

Macey set her drink under the counter. "Derek. You told me I could hire people. I just hired one."

He stared at the back of her head as she greeted a guy at the counter and took his order.

Gus tipped his head, drawing Derek over. "I thought you trusted her."

"I do." No hesitation on that.

"Then get over it. Go make a drink."

"I'm over it."

"I'd take a refill." Gus pushed his empty cup toward Derek.

"In your dreams." Derek tossed the cup in the trash. "How 'bout some nachos?"

"If this place doesn't make a profit, you're entirely to blame."

"I can live with that," Gus said. "Long as I get my nachos."

Andie was standing in the doorway to the back room. "Gotcha covered."

Derek shook his head at her uncharacteristic willingness to please, then turned back to Gus. "What is it with you and women? They act like your groupies."

"I'm handsome," Gus said.

Derek choked as he took a drink.

"I smile at 'em. You should smile more. Then they'll pay attention to you."

"You assume I want their attention. Things are much easier without it."

"Maybe. But not nearly as fun," Gus said.

Damn good thing Derek wasn't looking for fun.

CHAPTER SIX

LATER THAT NIGHT, Derek was reminded that while *he* wasn't looking for fun, Macey might be. And that she was perfectly capable of attracting male attention, especially with that sexy little tee and those shorts that showed off her legs. They weren't supermodel mile-long or anything—she was almost a foot shorter than him— but they were nice legs nonetheless. With just the right amount of curves and muscles and softness. Not that he was interested for himself. But he had no trouble seeing why other guys might be.

He'd not had to worry about anyone but himself for the past few months, but dammit, now that she was here he couldn't help worrying about her. Or rather, the men who pursued her.

Derek had witnessed more than a handful of guys flirting with her as she took their orders, delivered their cheese fries, grabbed their bottles of beer. For the most part, she was good at being friendly but noncommittal. She had a sway to her hips, though, that he was sure she wasn't aware of. He wished he could say the same for all the men in the place.

These two guys now, for example. Derek saw them come in, watched them when they spotted Macey and could tell they were interested in her as they took the last two available seats at the bar.

"Macey, what's up?" one of them said.

How the hell did they know her?

She walked over to them with a big smile, and Derek moved closer.

"What are you guys doing here?" Macey asked them.

"Looking for you," the second one said.

"Thought we'd check the place out. Haven't been here since it reopened," the first guy said.

Derek stepped next to Macey. "Need anything?" he asked her.

"Derek, this is Evan Drake and Clay Marlow. They live in the same building as me."

He nodded at them.

"They're local firefighters," she added, and he could tell by her tone she was anxious to gauge his reaction to that announcement.

Derek took his time in acknowledging her statement. He straightened and happened to spot Andie peeking around the doorway of the kitchen at that moment. She appeared to be sizing up Macey's firefighters. Scratch that...they weren't *Macey's* anything.

"Who's the brunette?" the guy Macey had introduced as Clay asked, nodding toward Andie.

"Resident rebel without a cause," Derek said. "Andie's our Harley-riding cook-bartender."

"One of those, huh? Sounds like trouble." Clay nodded and did his best to act indifferent, but Derek saw him glance one more time at her. "You the one Macey mentioned was with the Dallas Fire Department?"

He didn't like Macey telling people his business—especially *that* business—to people he didn't know. But there wasn't much he could say to her now without drawing undue attention to it. "Sure am," he confirmed.

"You quit?" Evan asked. There was interest and curiosity in his tone, no censure.

"Came down here to run this place for my retired uncle," Derek said.

"We could use you at the station," Clay suggested. "Seems like we've always got a spot open."

Macey was watching him too closely.

"I'm working this place seven days a week," he said, feigning regret. "There's no way I could do it."

"Maybe when we hire a few more people," Macey said.

Derek was glad as hell to see two women step up to the bar. Without acknowledging Macey's grand idea, he moved toward them, forced a smile and took their order.

IT WAS AFTER MIDNIGHT and Andie had left for the night. Derek was in back serving up some seviche when Macey stuck her head in the room. "Could you get me two more of those?" she asked, motioning toward the paper tray in his hand.

"Macey," he said before she could return to the front. "Watch yourself with those two."

She paused. "Evan and Clay? They're harmless, Dare."

"The one on the left wants you."

"They're my neighbors. That's all."

"Don't be naive."

She shook her head as if he was out of his mind, and hurried to the cash register.

Maybe he *was* out of his mind. That they were firefighters was about the only thing keeping him from asking them to leave. Most firefighters were honorable guys, but still, he knew plenty who enjoyed reaping the benefits of the firefighter image. They went through women faster than most people went through potato chips. Macey wasn't like that, had never been the type to date casually. Come to think of it, he hadn't ever been aware of her dating at all. She hadn't had any long-term relationships that he remembered. All the more reason the guy at the bar needed to leave her alone, honorable or not.

The two stayed until closing. When Derek and Macey walked out and he locked up, they were sitting at one of the outdoor tables.

"Aren't you guys out past your bedtime?" she asked, smiling.

"We're waiting for you," Evan said. "Thought we'd walk you home. Keep you safe."

Derek didn't need to look at him—he could hear the guy's grin.

"I'll walk you home," he told Macey.

"I'll be fine," she replied. "You live the other way."

"I want to. I owe you from the other night."

"You don't owe me anything...but suit yourself."

Damn straight he would.

He double-checked all the shutters and shoved the keys into the deep pocket of his cargo shorts. He and Macey joined the other two. She started toward the sand.

"We could take the street, you know," Derek said. "It's a shorter route."

"But it has no view." Macey sounded energetic, as if she hadn't been working for the past fourteen hours. "How can you live on an island and not want to take in the beach every chance you have?"

He knew his answer—that he barely noticed the beach—wasn't what she wanted to hear, so he just followed her and the others down the stairs.

DEREK WAS ACTING SO strangely tonight. Macey knew he was concerned that she shouldn't trust Evan and Clay, but she was a good judge of character. They were reliable. Safe. They wouldn't hurt her. Evan was a flirt, yes, but that's just how he was. Clay was more straightforward. Both were friendly, and she liked listening to their banter.

She supposed she should be glad Derek took notice of anything, even if his opinion of her neighbors was off base. His interest tonight was much better than his ongoing apathy and weariness. She also couldn't deny the thrill she still got from his protectiveness, even though it was only meant in friendship.

"So how long you going to do the bar thing?" Evan asked Derek as they walked along the sand in a wide-spread row.

"As long as I need to," he said. "My uncle signed it over to me, but he's there every day checking up on things."

"Are you done with firefighting for good?" Clay asked.

Derek didn't answer right away. "Done with it for now. I needed the break."

Both Clay and Evan nodded as if they understood, and Macey wondered if they'd ever suffered a tragedy anything like Derek had. What were the chances of trying to fight the fire that killed your girlfriend? She knew firefighters saw too much loss, more catastrophes than any person should have to witness, and she couldn't imagine what it took to handle that. She certainly didn't have it in her. Their job made living in an underdeveloped country seem like child's play.

"Well, if you ever change your mind, give us a call, man," Evan said.

"I'll keep that in mind. I've got my hands full trying to keep Gus happy for now."

"I know a little bit about trying to keep the family happy. They can be pains." Evan's affection for his family came through despite the complaint, though.

"Families are right up there alongside women for being pains," Clay said. "No offense, Macey."

"What do you know about women?" Evan asked. "You haven't been on a date in ages."

"I grew up with a houseful of sisters."

"You should ask the Harley girl out," Evan said.

"Not interested. I need a Harley girl like I need another sister."

"You sure checked her out a lot for not being interested."

"Here we are." Macey broke in as they crossed the street to their building. "Home sweet home…away from home. Anyone need a drink or a Ding Dong?"

"Ding Dongs? That's my cue to call it a night," Clay said. "Nice to meet you, Derek."

"I never mix beer and Ding Dongs myself," Evan added.

Macey laughed and waved as they headed to their apartment. "So?" she asked Derek, trying hard not to care if he said no.

"I'll take you up on the drink. You can keep the junk food."

"Like your meals at the bar are so much healthier. When's the last time you had a home-cooked meal?"

"Couldn't even tell you," he said in a disinterested tone.

"I'm no gourmet, but maybe one night I'll cook and force it down your throat."

"Promises, promises."

"The challenge would be prying you from your hidey-hole at the bar."

"It's not my hidey-hole. It's my job."

Restraining herself from arguing, she unlocked the door and he followed her inside.

"You really didn't have to do the manly man thing, walking me home."

"Wanted to."

"Why didn't you tell them why you're taking a break?" she asked as she went to the kitchen and got him a glass of ice water, since she still didn't have anything else. She helped herself to her chocolate fix and carried the glass to the living room.

"Why would I?"

She ripped the plastic off the Ding Dong and shrugged. "Because they can relate? Because they would understand?"

He set the glass aside, untouched, and paced away from her. On the other side of the small room, he faced the wall, rubbed his temples. "It's hard as hell to admit out loud that I'm not up to the task of saving people, Mace. But I'm not. So damn...not."

Macey had to fight the urge to go to him, to touch him. His posture told her to stay away, and she knew him well enough to recognize how hard it had been for him to say that.

"Have you ever thought that maybe it would be good to force yourself to go back to it? Maybe the extreme focus firefighting demands would help you."

"I don't have it in me to focus on anything other than a drink here and a hamburger there. That'd be a catastrophe waiting to happen."

She set her chocolate cake down on the end table, unable to stay away from him any longer. When she put her hands on his shoulders, though, he flinched.

"Don't."

Macey jumped back, startled by his harsh tone, even though she'd known full well he wouldn't want her to try to comfort him in any way.

"Please." He turned, but still didn't look at her. "I have to go."

She closed her eyes and let him walk out of her apartment.

No matter how hard she tried, she couldn't push the sting of his rejection away. What was she doing here? Why was she fighting this battle when he didn't want her help, didn't want her around?

Maybe they'd both be better off if she just went back to Dallas and got on with her life. This mission of hers seemed more ill-advised and hopeless every day.

CHAPTER SEVEN

MACEY'S PITY PARTY was over by the time she popped out of bed at seven the next morning. She had too much to do to feel sorry for herself for long. And when she stepped back from her conversation with Derek the night before, she knew he hadn't intended to hurt her. It was nothing personal. It was all about him and the grief and sadness that were burying him.

She threw on some capri sweats and a comfy old tee and drove to the coffee shop she'd spotted several blocks away. Normally she'd walk, just to enjoy the day, but she wanted to get started on work for her nonprofit this morning. She was also tossing around ideas for a business plan for The Shell Shack, even though Derek hadn't asked her to. She knew his response to something so formal would be an eye roll or a head shake. But it was the way Macey worked best. Everything accounted for, noted on paper. That was the way to succeed, and though Derek didn't currently care about much, she knew he wanted the bar to do well for his uncle's sake.

The coffee shop was jumping. She ordered a large mocha with extra chocolate syrup, and couldn't pass up a slice of cinnamon coffee cake, as well. She took them to go and hurried back to her apartment. When she pulled into the parking lot, she spotted Clay squatting next to a dark blue oversize truck, shining the wheel rims. A hose stretched from behind the eight-plex they lived in, and a sponge, a bucket and a couple of cloths were scattered near him.

"Morning," Macey said as she walked past.

"You're up early. I thought bartenders slept half the day away."

"Guess I'm a novice. You're off again today? Don't they ever make you work?"

"Got a twenty-four tomorrow morning. We work every third day."

"Ah, the luxury," Macey joked, fully aware of how taxing a shift could be for them. She had run into Derek post-shift a few times when she'd been home from school. The danger he and his fellow firefighters willingly put themselves in on a daily basis never failed to awe her. That was Derek—concerned about others, protective to a fault, willing to do whatever it took to get the job done. All reasons she cared so much about him and always would. Even though he was almost unrecognizable right now.

DEREK WAS IN THE SPARE bedroom that served as his home gym, bench-pressing weights, when his cell phone rang in the other room. There was no one he wanted to talk to—in fact, he was surprised to hear the sound at all, it'd been so long since he'd actually left the phone on. He let it ring.

Lowering the weight, he swore as the ringing continued.

It finally quieted and he grabbed his towel from the floor and ran it over his face. His body screamed at him, which was the result he was after, the reason he pushed himself so hard every workout. Pain. He craved the pain because it could pull him out of his sorry-ass mental state for a good hour, make him forget everything else. He'd run an extra mile this morning and added weight to all his rotations on the machine, and he was feeling it now. The burn in every part of him, every cell. *Bring it on.*

The blasted phone started up again and he whipped the towel to the floor. That'd teach him to leave the damn thing on.

He went to the bedroom and picked it up. The number on the display wasn't familiar. Relieved it wasn't his family, he pushed the talk button. If he'd remembered the date, he never would've answered.

"Derek? This is James. Julie's brother."

Derek braced himself against the shakiness and nausea that started up. He'd recognized the voice immediately. They'd watched *The Mummy* together at Julie's parents' house on Thanksgiving last year, just weeks before the fire. He hadn't spoken to James since her funeral.

He didn't want to speak to him now.

"Hello?" James said.

Derek gave serious consideration to hanging up.

"Derek. You there?"

"Yeah." Derek's voice sounded rusty in his own ear. "What's up, James?"

It was James's turn to hesitate. "I was just thinking

about her. Figured you probably were, too, since it's her birthday and all. Missing her. You know?"

Derek's throat clogged with emotion. "Yeah." Damn it all, he hadn't realized it was her birthday. June 4.

"She'd be twenty-eight today," James continued.

"Yeah." What else could he possibly say? That maybe if he'd tried harder she'd still be here to celebrate?

"You doing anything in honor of her birthday?"

Derek rubbed his fingers back and forth over his eyes, where a throbbing pain now centered. "Just working. Maybe I'll have a shot for her." Or a bottle.

"I was thinking of going out for a triple-dip cone from Coneheads."

Julie's favorite dessert. From her favorite hangout, near her apartment in Dallas.

Rocky road on top, mint chocolate chip in the middle, Heath crunch on the bottom.

"You should do that," he managed to say into the phone. "Hey, James, I need to get to work."

"Yeah, man, I know. Just thought I'd say hi."

"Later."

Derek pushed the end button and leaned his head against the bedroom wall. He'd wanted pain and now he had it in spades. Rushing over him like sheets of torrential rain that soaked him clear through. He was drowning, fighting for oxygen. His chest seemed filled with a swirling blackness and cold, dark grief.

Back at Christmastime, he'd toyed with the idea of proposing to Julie, but had decided her birthday would be better…less distracting. Today. He would've been engaged today.

The blackness boiled inside him, begging for release. He lurched around and punched the bedroom wall with everything he had as he swore a long stream of the vilest words he could think of. And that did about as much good for his pain as a dog raising a leg and pissing on a four-alarm fire.

THE MORNING FLEW BY. Macey had arranged to meet Ramon, the new guy, at eleven to start training before the lunch rush—which was amusing, really, since she was still learning the job herself. At ten-fifteen, she dragged herself away from a rough draft of the business plan for The Shell Shack. She'd become instantly engrossed in the challenge and was excited about the bar's prospects. Once they hired more people, she'd start implementing little changes here and there that would help Derek and make the business more profitable. She could set a lot in motion in the weeks she was here.

She dried her hair somewhat and clipped it up on her head, knowing with the humidity it'd still be damp at midnight. She quickly pulled on another pair of new shorts she'd bought with her mom when she'd first arrived home from Asia. They still felt way too short, but her mom had insisted they looked great on her and that short was in. Macey hadn't ever been much of a fashion bug, but after being gone for two years with little connection to the rest of the world, she admitted her wardrobe had fallen even more out of style than usual.

She eyed the bright red halter top hanging in the closet, but chose to layer a couple of tanks instead. The halter felt too revealing whenever she tried it on, even though some might say it was modest.

Stuffing ankle socks and tennis shoes into a bag, she slipped on some sandals and rushed out the door, determined to walk and enjoy the late-morning sun on the way to her very long shift. She couldn't figure out how Derek could work these hours day in and day out. Her first objective was to hire people he could trust so she could force him to take a day off each week.

The sky was cloudless and the sun beat down on her. Clusters of people dotted the sand—families with young children, teen girls and leather-skinned elderly couples working on their tans.

Macey watched for the first sight of the straw-roofed bar down the beach. When she finally spotted it, weird things happened to her insides, all because she knew Derek was there. This time it wasn't just anticipation of seeing him, though. Doubt made her drag her feet.

He really didn't want her here. In essence, he'd sent that message when he'd refused to let her stay with him. And last night he'd made it clear yet again that he didn't want her to interfere. Didn't want to do anything to get over his grief.

Who was she to try to break through that steel wall he'd erected? She wasn't special to him, regardless of her feelings for him, which, she realized, had only deepened in the few days she'd been here. Never mind her determination to keep them in check, or his efforts to push her away. If she wasn't careful she'd make a fool of herself, trying so hard to help a man who didn't want any help.

It wouldn't be the first time she'd made a fool of herself, though. She really had no alternative but to stay and keep trying to get through to Derek. Because she couldn't stand to leave when he was, well, like he was. He would hurt her along the way and she'd just have to deal with it. She could nurse her wounds later.

When she walked into the bar a few minutes later, though, she was surprised to find only Andie and Ramon, who really did look like an eighteen-year-old kid instead of the twenty-three years his application said he was. About a dozen customers were waiting around the bar to be served. She jumped into action and told Ramon to shadow her.

"Where is he?" she asked Andie as they stood side by side mixing drinks. Today Andie looked just like the Harley girl she was, sporting a bandanna to keep her long hair back, and a tee with a freaky skull design on it.

"I figured you'd know. I haven't seen him."

"Has he ever been late before?"

"What do you think?"

"He's never late," Macey said. She told Ramon what to ring up, and handed him the two fuzzy navels. "Have you tried to call him?"

"His phone's not on," Andie said.

"Fabulous." But her sarcasm was out of pure frustration. Worry niggled at her.

Her stomach was churning almost two hours later

when the flow of customers finally slowed down and Derek still hadn't appeared.

"I have to go find him," she told Andie, who'd just returned from wiping the tables clean. "Can you two cover me?"

Andie frowned at Ramon.

"We'll be fine," he said, sending Andie a goofy grin. "I can draw a mean beer."

Macey stifled a laugh. Ramon had a crush on the resident bad girl. Andie didn't even hint at a smile, which was how she was, Macey had learned. *Sunshiny* and *Andie* weren't words used in the same sentence unless you were talking about the weather.

"Go now," Andie stated. "The dinner rush will kill us if you're not here."

"I'll be back before that," Macey said, not allowing herself to think about the possibility that she might not find Derek before then.

"You can take my car," Ramon offered.

"I was going to walk. It's not far."

He tossed her his keys. "It's the blue Lincoln parked on the street. A big boat. Can't miss it."

Macey took his keys and, before leaving, grabbed the book she'd stowed under the counter a couple of days ago. She handed it to Ramon. "Study up."

"*The Bartender's Bible*. Sweet. Thanks."

"Are you going yet or what?" Andie asked impatiently.

Macey hurried to the street and glanced around. She spotted the Lincoln with no trouble. It was hard to miss, about twice as long as any other vehicle around and a nauseating powder-blue with a dent in the side. Probably almost as old as she was.

The door was unlocked—no one would try to steal this beast—so she climbed in and put the keys in the ignition. Surprisingly, it started right up and she pulled out onto the street. She hoped she could find a regular parking place at Derek's. Parallel parking this thing would take her a week.

Thankfully, there was a spot, and—double bonus— Derek's black pickup was parked right next to it. Maybe he'd just overslept and her worry was for nothing.

CHAPTER EIGHT

MACEY WENT TO Derek's door and knocked, then tried the knob without waiting. As before, it opened.

"Dare? Are you here?"

She glanced into his bedroom, not expecting to see his legs stretched out on the floor near the door. Her heart skipped a beat when she did. "Derek!"

"What?" His tone, impatient, annoyed, startled her.

She entered the room and stared down at him in his exercise shorts and tattered red muscle shirt, propped against the wall. He looked like hell. His hair was disheveled, and he was slouched so much it had to hurt. His eyes were bloodshot.

"Are you okay?" She knelt next to him and touched his cheek.

He flinched away from her. "Don't."

"What's going on? You're hours late for work and you look like you've been drunk for the past week."

"Don't I wish."

He had yet to make eye contact. Macey's adrenaline was pumping and she scooted closer to him, until her knees ran into his thigh. "What *happened?*"

Then she spotted what he held. The photo of Julie.

"Oh," she said quietly, her heart breaking. She longed

to climb on his lap and wind her arms around him, to tell him everything was going to be okay, but...

She'd heard all the usual trite phrases at age ten, when her father had died. They were just empty lines people tossed out when they didn't know what else to say. She'd promised herself never to use those on anyone.

She picked up his left hand and lightly traced his fingers. She'd never really noticed how big his hands were before, how strong. As she wove her fingers with his, she felt the calluses from years of work, saw the white scars and noticed several recent scratches. Then she glanced at his right hand. The knuckles were scraped and bloody. Starting to bruise.

"Did you get in a fight?" she asked.

"With the wall. I won."

Macey spotted a gaping hole above them, a couple of feet to the left. "What'd the wall do to you?" She looked again at his swelling knuckles. "Are you sure you won?"

She might as well have been talking *to* the wall for all the response she got. Maybe hole number one could use a friend. Rolling her eyes at the stupidity of punching walls, she stood.

"Derek. What the hell is wrong with you? I know you're grieving, but what happened today?"

He sat there in silence for so long she wanted to kick a reaction out of him.

"Today's her birthday," he finally said, his voice so quiet and full of anguish that Macey barely heard him. "I'd planned on asking her to marry me."

Macey had no words. She sat down heavily, straddling his legs just above his knees, giving no thought to the contact now, too wrapped up in trying to somehow assuage his pain even though she knew she couldn't. She took both of his hands in hers and squeezed them.

Derek raised his chin and stared at the ceiling. Swallowed hard. "Sorry I skipped out on work."

"We did okay. But I was worried. I wish you'd told me what you were up against. I would've understood."

He met her gaze head-on. "I forgot it was her birthday, Mace. She's only been gone for five months and I'm already moving on, acting like I don't care. Forgetting the date I was going to propose."

"You're not acting like you don't care. I can tell you care, can tell you're mourning her in every single thing you do."

"I forgot her *birthday*."

"No offense, but I've seen no evidence of you moving on, Dare. You've practically stopped living."

He shook his head and looked away.

"You know something? There's no right way to get through this. When my dad died, I thought there was. Thought I was supposed to talk about him to people who paid respect, *avoid* talking about him to my mom. I even thought there was a timeline. After a month, I should've felt better, right?"

"You were just a kid."

"Oh, so there's a *What to Do When Someone Dies* handbook for adults now?" She narrowed her eyes, frustrated that she couldn't help, that he was so hard on himself. "You know, I can't tell you how to grieve. But I can tell you that you need to quit beating yourself up. Quit worrying about what you do or don't feel."

"Bossy."

"We've established that. And while I'm at it, one more thing. Quit punching walls, because I seriously think you lost on that. Your hand looks terrible."

"It'll be fine."

She stood. "You should take the rest of the day off."

He ran his beat-up hand through his hair and flinched, which told Macey his knuckles hurt worse than he was letting on. "I need to work."

"The world won't stop spinning if you take one night off."

He rose from the floor slowly. "I can't stand being in this place for the rest of the night. I'll come to work."

That she could understand. "Okay. If that's the case, get your butt in the shower. You smell like a gym. And call Gus. He's worried."

He stared stubbornly at her and then lifted the muscle shirt over his head, revealing that sculpted chest that had been burned into her mind since she'd watched him sleeping. Before Macey could react, he lowered his shorts.

"Going to stay for the rest?" he asked.

She couldn't help it; she looked down, thinking he'd surely left his underwear on. But holy cripes…nope. She averted her eyes, not quickly enough. He was staring at her, saw her reaction, which had to be all over her face because she'd never been able to hide a thing. Her cheeks warmed.

Derek's lips twitched into a humorless near smile. "Careful who you boss around."

He turned away and walked to the bathroom and, Lord help her, she couldn't *not* check out his butt. Just for a second. Long enough to see that it was as beautiful and perfectly toned as the rest of his body. She whipped her eyes back up and wanted to sink through the floor when she realized he'd looked over his shoulder and again caught her staring at him. She hurried out of the room to wait at a safe range. Like maybe Alaska.

DEREK HADN'T EXPECTED to be turned on by Macey's reaction to his nakedness.

What the living, breathing hell was wrong with him that he could be aroused by the interest in her eyes…on his girlfriend's birthday, less than six months after she'd died?

He hated himself at that instant, hated his weakness, hated the reality that the woman he'd loved had died instead of him. He was such a bastard.

He stepped into the shower before the water heated, letting the cold pound down on his aching body. Grabbing the bar of soap, he scrubbed like the devil.

"THOUGHT YOU WERE bringing Mr. Personable back with you," Andie said when Macey walked into the bar.

"He's on his way. He's…showering." She busied herself by picking up a towel and wiping down the side of the bar so the other woman wouldn't notice her blush.

When Andie just stared pointedly at her, she wiped harder.

"Mary Ann okay?" Ramon asked as he came in from the back room.

Macey stopped what she was doing. "Mary Ann?"

"The car. Only woman I've got right now." He cocked a suggestive eyebrow toward Andie, who scowled at him.

"Mary Ann's fine. Thanks for letting me use it—her." Macey attempted a smile. "I like the name."

"So glad the *car* is okay," Andie said drily. "What's with Derek?"

"Just a bad day." Macey didn't know if he'd told Andie anything about Julie, and wasn't sure it was her place to share it.

"You're acting strange. What happened?" Andie was watching her too carefully.

"Just worried about him." That was personal enough. She wasn't about to mention seeing him naked or her embarrassing reaction.

"Ramon, go wipe down the outside tables, would you?" Once he'd gone outside, Andie lowered her voice. "He's like a puppy dog, following me around. I'll never forgive you for hiring him."

Macey chuckled. "He's harmless."

"Easy for you to say. Eager beavers are not my type."

"What is your type?" she asked as they prepped the place for the evening rush.

"Don't have a type. I like being on my own, accountable to no one. I don't stay in one place for long."

"You've been here for a while, haven't you?"

"A few weeks. I'm getting antsy."

"Does Derek know you might up and leave anytime?"

"I told him that when he hired me. But I'll try to give you some warning so you can hire someone."

"Add it to the list. I need about four more people already. I'm not getting enough response from the fliers or the sign in the window."

"There was a guy in here earlier asking about a job. He managed a bar in Wisconsin. Down here for the summer, maybe more."

"Did you get his name?"

Andie dug in the pocket of her jeans, which fit her like a second skin. She pulled out a business card and handed it to Macey. "I told him you'd call tomorrow."

"Thanks. Did he set off any creep alarms?"

"No, but then my creep alarms may not be as sensitive as yours."

Macey tucked the card into her pocket and turned to help the group that were stepping up to the bar, just as Derek appeared. The customers were studying one of the paper menus from the stack by the register, so she watched him walk over to the other register to run the report and clear out the drawer. He finally glanced her way and their eyes met. His jaw tightened and he looked away.

Nothing personal, she reminded herself, though it was difficult not to take it that way. The woman in front of her started to order, so Macey had to put Derek out of her mind.

It wasn't until many hours later that she was able to think about him again. She'd accepted a ride home from Andie on her motorcycle—a first for Macey—and barely managed to shed her sweaty clothes before withering into bed. The long shifts were exhausting enough, but the scene at Derek's had taken a lot out of her, too.

He hadn't spoken to her other than what was demanded by the job, but the bar had been the busiest she'd seen it and the receipts for the day confirmed that. There hadn't been much chance to say anything, anyway. However, it hadn't escaped her notice that he'd been simmering with anger the entire evening. He had no reason to be mad at her, she told herself yet again. He was the one who'd stripped down.

Don't think about it anymore.

As she tried to go to sleep, she couldn't shake the image of Derek's naked body.

It was going to be a long night.

CHAPTER NINE

DEREK WOKE UP to the sound of his condo door opening and shutting. He rubbed the sleep out of his eyes and sat up in the chair as Macey came barreling down the hall toward the living room.

"When are you going to learn to lock your door?" she asked.

"Soon, if you keep walking in on me," he mumbled to himself. It'd been a week since Julie's birthday, the day he'd missed the first half of work. Macey had backed off after that. Either she sensed he needed to be alone or she was just preoccupied by all the hiring she'd done. She was taking over the bar piece by piece and, frankly, he was glad. It needed help and he couldn't give it. All he could do was show up and pour drinks.

"What are you doing here?" he asked. "What time is it?"

"Seven-thirty. We're going out."

"We? Got a mouse in your pocket?" he asked as she crossed the living room and opened the blinds, letting in the bright sunlight. He could see, though, that there was no mouse in her pocket. There was nothing in her pocket. She wouldn't be able to fit *anything* in the microscopic pocket of her microscopic shorts.

Since when did she look like *that?* he wondered, letting his eyes roam over the red top that showed off a strip of skin at her waist and bared most of her back. Macey had apparently come out of her shell sometime when he wasn't looking.

"You are going to get up, take a shower and dress. I've brought coffee and doughnuts."

"How about if you leave the coffee and doughnuts and go away."

"Nice try, but you're not scaring me off by being mean."

"I thought that was a lot more polite than telling you to get the hell out."

"Glad to see your thoughtfulness isn't completely gone. Now." She pointed toward his bedroom.

"Why?"

"I'm taking you somewhere."

"Where?"

"You'll see when we get there."

Derek sat back in the chair. "You may have noticed I'm not in the mood to play games lately."

"This isn't a game."

"Then tell me what we're doing."

"If I tell you, will you get your butt in the shower?"

He didn't want to think about the last time he'd gotten his butt in the shower with her here. "Yes."

"A dolphin cruise."

He stared, waiting for her to laugh and say she was joking. She crossed her arms and stared right back at him.

"Shower."

"You're kidding about the dolphin cruise, right?"

"Not in the least."

"Macey. I have a bar to run."

"Actually, I've kind of been running it for you, and I've scheduled people to cover until noon. They won't let you in before that. Consider it an employee revolt."

"What makes you think—"

"We made a deal, Derek. You can bark at me all you want later, but you're not going to work until noon. You can either stay in your lonely condo and brood or you can come with me and shut me up."

"That'll be the day." He stood but made no move toward his bedroom. Macey took his arm and tried pulling him in that direction. When she figured out she couldn't budge him, her shoulders drooped.

"Will you do this for me, please?" she asked softly.

"Do what for you?"

"I want to see the dolphins. I haven't had the chance to do anything fun or touristy since I've been here, and I just want to do this."

"Why do you need me?" he asked suspiciously.

"Because I can't watch dolphins all alone."

He stared at her, sure she was playing him, but the look on her face was earnest and a little bit sad.

"Please?" she repeated.

He knew he'd been a terrible friend since she'd set foot on the island. He could do this one thing. Even if she was feeding him a line of crap. "You're sure they've got the bar covered?"

"Andie's there, Ramon's there and so is Kevin the Great," she said, referring to the newest hire, the veteran bar manager from up North. He was one of three more new hires Macey had made in the past week. "They'll be fine and we'll get there in time for the big lunch crowd." She pegged him with those green eyes. "Trust me, Derek."

He gritted his teeth and headed for the shower, muttering the whole way that he was a sucker and he knew it.

"LOOK AT ALL OF THEM!" Macey said in awe.

She and Derek stood on the top level of the double-decker boat, leaning along the front railing. They were crowded into the corner, near all the other passengers straining to get a glimpse of the dolphins, but they had an excellent view so she wasn't complaining.

There must have been a dozen dolphins out there, just a few feet away. She'd seen them on TV and at zoos, but never in the wild. It was incredible to watch them so close, playing tag with the boat. Macey stole a glance at Derek and saw he was actually smiling. Such a small thing, that smile, but a huge step.

He looked down at her. "They're amazing, aren't they?"

Macey nodded and turned her attention back to the pod. The captain had stopped the engine and the boat was drifting in the bay, close to where it and the gulf joined. Other boats sped by, trailing monstrous wakes. A particularly large wave reached and rocked them, sending Macey crashing into Derek's side.

"I told you to lay off the liquor," he said as he put his arm around her to steady them both against the high railing.

Macey gasped. "Was that a funny? I didn't know you still had it in you."

"I take it back. Don't know what came over me." But he was smiling. And his arm remained at her waist, which made the moment all the more magical. Even if it was one-sided magic.

"You think we should call Andie?" Derek asked after the dolphins had swum away and he and Macey had taken their seats again.

"What for?"

He shrugged. "To make sure everything's okay."

"Everything's fine. And if it isn't, what are you going to do? You're on a boat in the middle of the bay."

Derek bounced his knees up and down restlessly. "I'm not used to not being there."

Macey squeezed his forearm gently. "Don't take this the wrong way, Dare, but the beer will flow without you."

He stared at her for several seconds and finally cracked another grin. They were going for a record today with the smiles. "When you put it like that, I sound like an idiot."

Macey laughed. "You're not an idiot. You're dedicated to the bar just like you used to be dedicated to firefighting."

He looked away, out over the side of the boat toward the mainland.

"Do you miss it?" Macey asked tentatively.

Derek shook his head. "I don't think about it."

"Maybe you should."

His gaze penetrated hers. "Are you trying to ruin this?"

"You're right. Forget I said anything. This has been fun. Next time I think we should try surfing or sand sculpture lessons."

"You sound like a tourist brochure."

"I am on vacation, technically."

He chuckled. "Hate to tell you this, but most people don't work a full-time job on vacation."

"The bar is a fun job."

He raised an eyebrow.

"You don't enjoy it?"

"It passes the time."

"That's all? You spend sixteen hours a day there and it passes the time?"

"Like you said, it's pouring beer and mixing liquor. Not something I always dreamed of doing."

"But you do it for Gus."

"Do I need a better reason?"

She shook her head. What he was saying just confirmed for Macey that he needed to get back to firefighting. He might not be ready yet, and that was fine, but she would do what she could to get him ready. Somehow.

They rode in silence the rest of the way back to the marina, engrossed in the sights and the captain's entertaining narration. When they disembarked, Macey dragged him into the gift shop.

"This is all tourist crap, Mace."

"Tourist crap happens to be exactly what I'm looking for." She wanted a souvenir of the day. It was the first fun time she and Derek had actually spent together in years. She wanted to remember forever the magical feeling she'd had, with his arm around her, watching the dolphins.

"Here we go," she said, picking out two plastic dolphin key chains.

"Charming," Derek said when she held them up. "Last of the big spenders."

"My boss doesn't pay me enough." She took the souvenirs to the counter to pay for them. Rejecting the paper bag the cashier offered her, she immediately started transferring her keys to one of the dolphins. Then she held out her hand to Derek. "Keys, please."

"What? No. You're not putting that thing on my keys."

"I am. That way you won't lose them. Hand 'em over."

"I never lose them and I don't want a goofy dolphin hanging from them."

They arrived at her car and she unlocked the doors. "You really don't remember how to have fun, do you?" she said as they climbed in. She would grab his keys later, when he wasn't paying attention.

Derek scoffed. "I may be rusty but I feel confident saying a cheap plastic dolphin is not fun."

"Old man."

"Little girl. Next you'll be collecting Hello Kitty."

"I used to love Hello Kitty, thank you. Do you need to go home before heading to work?"

"I'm good. Let's make sure they haven't burned the place down."

Macey parked along the street outside the bar. "Derek," she said when he reached for the door handle.

He stopped and looked at her.

"Thanks for coming with me today. I loved it."

The corners of his mouth tilted upward. "You are so full of it. That wasn't for you at all."

"What do you mean?" she asked innocently.

"I mean you did that to drag me out of my pathetic existence."

"Me? I'd never do something like that." She couldn't keep from smiling herself. "Okay. Maybe a little. But I really was dying to see the dolphins. And I hate doing things like that alone."

He hesitated for several seconds. "It was fun." He said the words with such seriousness, as if it was a shameful confession.

"Next time we're totally doing the sand-castle lessons."

"Why would anyone want sand-castle lessons?"

"To learn how to build big, beautiful sand sculptures, of course."

"You're pushing your luck."

"Yeah, well, I've gotten good at that. Come on. We're late."

"Did you two have sex or something?"

Macey jumped, then looked around to make sure no one else had heard Andie but her. Derek was out on the patio cleaning up trash and wiping tables, thank goodness.

The crowd had thinned out considerably about an hour ago. It was just after midnight and they would most likely have one more rush on drinks between now and last call.

"What are you talking about?" Macey asked.

"I don't know, but it sounds worth hearing." Lauren was one of the new employees, a Texas A&M student who was spending the summer on San Amaro Island before her senior year. She'd just come out of the back room.

"He's been in a decent mood all day. I just wondered if you're the reason," Andie stated.

"I told you, we went on a dolphin cruise this morning," Macey said emphatically to both of them. "That's all."

"Right." Andie shook a drink she was mixing for a rail-thin woman who sat playing solitaire at the outer counter.

"Derek and I aren't... That wouldn't happen."

"You're getting flustered," Andie taunted.

"Your face is turning red," Lauren added, and Macey wondered why she'd hired females. A guy would never notice any of this.

"It's hot in here. Lauren, weren't you supposed to leave a few minutes ago?"

The student checked her watch and swore. "I'm outta here. See you Wednesday afternoon."

"See you," Macey said, and went to the back room to get a sleeve of plastic cups.

When she returned, Andie was handing change to her customer at the counter. "So?" she said when the woman walked away.

Macey had been hoping Andie would drop the subject. "You don't know what happened to him before he came here, do you?" she asked, deciding now was the time to tell some of Derek's past, if only to convince Andie they were not involved beyond friendship.

"He doesn't tell me and I don't ask."

"His girlfriend was killed in a fire." She made sure to say it quietly so no one else would overhear.

"Holy shit." Andie filled her cup with lemonade and added a shot of cherry syrup. "How long ago?"

"January."

Andie was quiet and Macey straightened the shelf of liquor bottles.

"She died?" Andie asked, after taking a gulp.

Macey nodded.

"And he was a firefighter?"

"He worked the fire that killed her. Another firefighter died trying to save her. The entire building collapsed on them."

Andie didn't say anything, just shook her head.

"What's up with the hen fest?" Derek asked as he walked behind the bar.

Uncharacteristically, Andie hurried to the kitchen without a word. Normally she wouldn't take the hen comment sitting down.

"What's with her?" Derek asked, still sounding much

more cheerful than Macey had heard him since she'd been on San Amaro.

She shrugged. "My guess is she's just ready to go home."

"She was supposed to leave at twelve, wasn't she? Go home, Andie!" he hollered back.

She appeared in the doorway. "Bite me. I'm leaving."

Macey laughed as she continued to organize the liquor bottles and clean the shelves under them.

All her tidying was for naught, because two hours later, when they finally kicked the last customer out to the patio so they could close up, the area behind the counter was a complete shambles.

"That little rush helped the day's sales," Macey said, staring at the war zone otherwise known as the back counter.

"Little rush? Word must've gone out that this was the last chance for alcohol this decade, the way they crowded in here." Derek totaled out the registers and Macey glanced over his shoulder to see the numbers. "At this rate I'll be able to retire in a week."

"Dream on," Macey told him. "We're low on everything. But that should very nicely cover all the supplies we need. We're getting a big delivery in the morning."

Derek stared at her. "I bow down. You are the goddess of all things business."

Macey felt herself blushing but loved the compliment. "No big deal," she said.

"No big deal? I don't bow down to just anyone. I couldn't do this without you."

His seriousness made her squirm.

"Derek?"

He pulled out the cash bag without looking at her. "Yeah."

"You'd do fine without me, so shut up." With that, she took the built-in line for soda water, aimed it at him and shot him in the side of the face, soaking his hair and getting soda water in his ear. She tried to keep her laughter to herself, and crossed her fingers that he was in a good enough mood not to explode, because, wow, she'd gotten him much wetter than she'd meant to.

He set the cash bag in the drawer and stood still, dripping. "You should *not* have done that." His voice was low and she couldn't tell if he was mad. "Start regretting it now, honey, because you're going down."

Macey ran to the back room, howling with laughter. Stupid move, as the back door was already padlocked. Derek cornered her and threw one arm around her middle, dragging her back to the front. Before she could figure out his intentions, he took the whipped cream spigot and squirted her. It was hooked up to a large tank, so he wouldn't run out anytime soon. As he coated her face, Macey closed her eyes, laughing so hard she couldn't get enough air to tell him to stop.

Finally he did stop, but not before she must've looked like a cream pie. She wiped her face off and flung the cream at him, nailing him in the head. They both stood there, cracking up and wiping the mess off themselves. Macey's sides hurt and she couldn't stand up straight.

"Missed some," Derek said when they'd calmed down a couple degrees. He wiped a splotch of whipped cream off her temple, smiling broadly. "I think white's your color."

She looked up into his eyes, which had more life in them than she'd seen since she got here. His smile slowly disappeared as he moved closer to her, and Macey's heart leaped to her throat. This wasn't really happening, was it? Was she reading him wrong?

Oh my, no, she wasn't.

Derek leaned in closer still and she could feel his breath on her lips. She didn't dare move. She shouldn't let this happen, but she had wanted it for so many years....

The touch of his lips was like cool seawater on a hot day. Something she needed, something she'd longed for for so long she didn't remember when she hadn't. The softness of his mouth was such a contrast to the hard body pressed up against her, his gentleness so unexpected from a man who'd always lived life hard. Her insides pooled and her legs threatened to give out.

She wrapped her arms around him, as much for support as to draw him even nearer. He pressed her backside into the counter with his aroused body, which helped her stay upright but sent her pulse into overdrive. Derek's tongue swirled inside her mouth and she met it with her own, exploring him, thrilling to the feel of him. He smelled like a mixture of whipped cream and man, and she would likely never forget it.

Derek broke the contact abruptly. She opened her eyes in silent question and he held her gaze for a long second before stepping back and turning away.

"What was that?" she said, trying to keep the tone light, trying to hide that he had just sent her world spinning off-kilter.

"That—" he walked across the room "—was a mistake."

Her heart plummeted. She felt as if someone had actually punched her in the middle.

"I'm sorry, Macey. I was totally out of line."

She wanted to argue.

She wanted to tell him it was the best hundred and twenty seconds of her life, better than anything she'd dreamed about over the past ten years. She wanted to say it was okay.

But it wasn't.

It so wasn't okay.

How had she let that happen? She was the stronger one here, the one who wasn't hurting, who wasn't in a weakened, grieving state. She'd come here knowing this could never happen, that it would never work out between them, and yet she'd let him kiss her. And she'd kissed him back like some desperate, needy idiot who would take whatever she could get, regardless of the consequences.

She nodded. "A mistake. On both our parts." She actually managed to sound strong. "Let's pretend it never happened." Even as she said it, she knew that kiss would be branded in her mind forever.

Well, so be it, but he didn't have to know that. As far as he knew, she regretted it as much as he did.

"Never happened," Derek repeated. "Good idea. Let's get this place cleaned up."

Just like that, he was over it. Macey was still shaking, still trying to wrap her brain around the fact that Derek had kissed her. *Her* Derek, after all these years, had kissed her and been turned on and totally into it, if only for a short moment. And now he was back to counting out the cash.

"I'll be back in a minute," she said, still managing to sound normal instead of inside out. She focused on the exit and only breathed when the cool middle-of-the-night breeze whispered over her on her way to the restroom on the other side of the patio.

Once inside, she closed herself in a stall and leaned against the wooden wall, wondering how she would ever pretend that kiss had never happened.

DEREK DIDN'T OFFER to see Macey home that night. The last twenty minutes they'd scrubbed, swept and mopped in silence. Other nights the quiet would've been companionable and comfortable, but tonight the air was tense. Electric.

He was such a goddamn ass. How could he kiss another woman? How could he allow himself to touch someone else?

As he drove his truck home, the cab seemed to be

devoid of oxygen, and by the time he pulled into his parking spot, sweat soaked his skin. He couldn't get out of there fast enough.

He let himself into the dark condo and didn't bother turning on any lights until he reached the spare bedroom, where he kept the weight machine. Ripping his shirt over his head, he started the most punishing workout he could devise, adding weight and reps to every damn exercise he could think of. Pain. He needed the pain. Deserved it.

Somehow the pain was easier than the guilt.

CHAPTER TEN

PRETENDING THE KISS HAD never happened became second nature over the course of the next week. Macey had been denying her feelings for so many years that this just fell into that category. Pure denial. At least when she was around Derek.

When she was at home by herself, reliving the kiss was fair game, to the extent that she wished she *could* forget about it. That would be preferable to the torture she was putting herself through.

Unfortunately, she'd cut back on her bar hours—she was working mostly eight-hour shifts instead of open to close—since she'd managed to hire five people now. While it was good for her to be away from Derek, that gave her free time. Thinking time. Time for her mind to wander. She was beginning to understand why he preferred to work day and night—not that her problem was anything compared to losing a loved one. But there was solace in being too busy to think.

Business at The Shell Shack was booming. The new hires had been trained, and Macey, Derek, Andie and Kevin were able to split supervisory duties so they could each work closer to forty hours. Not all of her work hours, thank goodness, were with Derek, but this evening they were closing together. To think, she'd begged him to hire her so she could be near him....

Macey was taking advantage of a lull to stock cups and napkins when someone spoke to her from a stool at the counter.

"It's our hero—*heroine*—in bartending clothes."

Evan's voice, becoming familiar now, made her smile. She turned to see him and Clay leaning on the counter.

"The usual?" she asked as she moved down the bar to them. They'd been in only twice before, but both times they'd gotten the same thing.

"I like that. Personalized service," Evan stated.

"Not bad. But I'll take a Coke instead of a beer," Clay said. "We start a twenty-four in the morning."

"One beer isn't going to hurt anything," Evan said. "The usual, please."

Macey noticed the way his eyes followed her. She was flattered by his attention. It wasn't every day a man who looked like *him* showed interest in her.

"You guys want anything to eat?" she asked as she set down a bottle of Bud and a Coke.

They both ordered burgers and cheese fries, and Macey went to give the order to Lauren.

As she was heading back in, Derek appeared in the doorway and blocked her way.

"Excuse me, Dare."

He just stared at her and didn't move.

"What is your problem?" she asked. They were busy enough that neither one of them had time to stand around, let alone both.

"You need to watch out for yourself," Derek said.

"What?"

He gestured with his head to the men behind him. "One of them is after you."

"After me?" Macey couldn't help laughing. "Do you think he'll turn into a stalker?"

"I think he's going to ask you out."

"Already did." With that, she removed Derek's arm from the door frame and walked past him, trying to stifle another laugh at his stunned expression. She hadn't planned on telling him, because it wasn't a big deal, but he'd asked for it.

The next ten minutes she avoided him by rushing from one customer to the next, and Derek was kept busy, as well. When she had to take another order to the back, he followed her.

"What did you say?" he demanded.

"Huh?"

"What did you tell him?"

"What did I tell who?" The order she'd just taken was from a woman.

"What did you tell the firefighter when he asked you out?"

Ahhh. He was still on that. A pointless little shiver of excitement coursed through her. "I told him no."

"Good." Derek scowled as he returned to his work.

Something about the set of his jaw irritated Macey. Who was he to butt in on her business? What if she had said yes to Evan?

Come to think of it, why hadn't she?

The obvious reason, futile though it was, stood right in front of her, mixing a tequila sunrise.

It didn't escape her that she was right back where she'd been during her last year of college. In love with Derek and turning down opportunities because of it.

She didn't feel a spark with Evan, but they could still have a good time on a date. As she'd pointed out to Derek numerous times, she was capable of taking care of herself, and she wasn't afraid to go out with Evan. At least then she could tell herself she wasn't waiting around for Derek and what would never be.

Macey decided before the night was over she would tell Evan she wanted to change her answer to a yes. Then she would officially be moving forward.

THINGS NEVER SEEMED TO GO as smoothly at the bar when Macey wasn't there. Today happened to be one of her few days off and they'd run out of several things, including change for the register. Minor problems that didn't happen when she was around.

It was just after 10:00 p.m. when Ramon again asked Derek for quarters, which hadn't materialized out of thin air in the hour since they'd run out. Derek growled as he added whipped cream to an icy strawberry daiquiri that deserved a miniature umbrella floating in it—another thing they'd run out of.

"Still no quarters, dude. Use dimes and nickels." As he turned and took the two steps to the counter to set the drink down, he spotted Macey entering the shack through the doorway to his left. His spirits rose, either because she might be able to get him quarters or maybe just because she was a friendly face in a sea of thirsty strangers. A heartbeat later, though, he frowned.

Trailing closely behind Macey was the firefighter who'd asked her out. The one she'd claimed to have turned down.

Evidently she'd lied, because there she was with him, and it was most definitely a date. She looked…God, she looked hot. She wore a short white dress that hugged her curves and showed off her tan, among other things. It wasn't indecent—she was well-covered—but it was eye-catching, and sent Derek's imagination into overdrive. Her heels added a good three inches to her height and made her legs look like a model's. Her hair hung down in big waves over her shoulders and back, and she wore more makeup than usual.

"Look at Macey," Lauren said with approval as she came up beside Derek. "Who is *that* she's with?"

"Her neighbor," Derek muttered, before helping the next customer. "Switch registers with me and take the line on the other side." He was damn well going to be the one to wait on Macey and her "non-date."

Macey smiled and flipped her hair behind her shoulder as Derek watched. No question, she was trying to impress this guy.

And unless the dude lacked a pulse, she was likely doing a hell of a job.

Derek's eyes were drawn to her repeatedly as he waited on the people in front of her. He told himself it was because he hadn't seen her dolled up for years. And frankly, she'd never looked quite like *that*.

When the customers before her were served, Macey stepped up to the counter and smiled. "Hey, Dare."

"Hey," he grunted.

"Been busy?"

"Slightly. What can I get you?"

Her smile slipped a notch. Sue the hell out of him if he wasn't as cheerful as her.

Evan had been talking to someone he apparently knew, standing a few feet away, and now he returned his attention to Macey, moving up beside her at the counter. He put his hand on the small of her back. "How's it going?" he said to Derek.

"Going." Derek had to fight to be civil. If the guy wasn't a firefighter, he wouldn't bother to try.

Macey's gaze narrowed in on Derek. "I'd like a strawberry margarita and a basket of cocktail shrimp, please."

"I'll have a double burger, loaded, cheese fries and a beer."

"Draw or bottle?" Derek asked.

"Bottle of Bud," Macey answered for him. Wasn't that just cozy that she knew his drink.

Her date nodded to another couple who came in as he dug out his wallet.

"What are you doing here?" Derek asked Macey. "It's your night off."

"Evan asked where I wanted to go for a drink and

this is about the only place I know. Besides, the food's decent."

Derek couldn't help but be mollified a little by the smile she gave him. "Plus I make a mean strawberry marg."

"That, too."

"Thanks," Derek said to Evan as he took his cash. "I'll bring it out to you in a couple."

And since he was so damn nice, he wouldn't even mess with the guy's food.

THE NIGHT WAS PERFECT for a romantic stroll. Nearly full moon, cloudless sky, relatively gentle waves rolling in, soft breeze rustling through Macey's hair.

No matter how hard she tried, though, she couldn't summon any romantic feelings for Evan.

There wasn't a thing wrong with him. Quite the opposite, actually—someone needed to fall in love with this man. Probably many women already had. Macey would be shocked if he hadn't left a path of broken hearts in his wake.

He was a decent conversationalist and had a great sense of humor. Then there were his looks and that body. He was striking in an everyday, athletic, quarterback way. With muscles to match.

Yet there was no spark when she looked at him, no desire to take him home and talk for hours and then do something altogether different.

She wished there was because the whole point of going out with him was to see if he could help her forget Derek.

If this man couldn't do it, there weren't likely many, if any, who could.

"There's something I need to ask you," Evan said as they strolled along the beach in the general direction of their apartment building, Macey carrying her heels. They'd stayed at The Shell Shack for much longer than they'd planned, talking their way through a couple more drinks.

"You make it sound serious," Macey said, hoping he would lighten up in response.

He didn't. He walked for several more moments before saying anything at all. "What's going on between you and the ex-firefighter? Derek, is it?"

"Derek. Nothing's going on." She nodded once with conviction.

"Macey. As the guy stuck in the middle, give me a little credit."

What could he possibly know? She always made a point of not showing how she felt about Derek. Well, except for the kiss, but that was just a giant error no one had witnessed. And Derek had initiated it, which made her feel not quite as exposed by it.

"What are you stuck in the middle of?" she asked.

"That's what I'm trying to find out. Were you two involved in the past?"

Only if you counted her dreams. "We're friends. Good friends. We grew up together. Our moms have co-owned a restaurant for years and that's how we met. When we were five. We've never been more than friends."

"That's a big explanation for a little question."

She hadn't considered it such a little question, but she supposed that was revealing in itself. "There's nothing between us," she insisted.

"I was right there. I'd have to be dead not to notice how he reacted to seeing you on a date with me."

"*I* must be dead then. How did he react?"

"He staked his claim."

"He doesn't have a claim." Her heart contradicted her words, constricting with the familiar ache.

"He's got…something. Feelings for you."

"Yes. Brotherly feelings. That's all." Just admitting it out loud was like a knife to the chest.

"So you're trying to tell me the cold shoulder he gave me was simply a don't-break-my-sister's-heart warning kind of thing?"

"Yes."

Again Evan didn't speak for several seconds. Then he shook his head. "You're wrong."

Jeez. This wasn't fair to Evan and she knew it. She stopped walking and he followed suit. "I care about him. Not as a brother. But it's all one-sided and I'm embarrassed to tell you that, and so sorry I went out with you when I care about someone else and there's really no hope of getting past it."

Evan studied her as he absorbed her words. She reached out and touched his forearm. "I'm sorry. I'd hoped that spending time with you could change the way I feel. You're so…" She felt her cheeks warming and hoped her blush wouldn't be visible in the dark, big moon or not. "You know you're good-looking."

A cocky grin spread across his face and he stood straighter. The grin faded quickly, though. "I'd be flattered if you weren't rejecting me. You're hard on a guy's ego."

Macey tried to keep a straight face. "I suspect you have enough ego to get through just fine."

"You hurt me with such cruel words," he mocked, making her laugh.

She pushed her hair behind her ear and started walking again, watching the white glimmer of shells beneath her feet until she and Evan angled off the beach and cut across the pavement toward their building. "You'll have a new woman next week."

"I was hoping for tomorrow. You must not think much of me, after all."

"If you take someone out tomorrow, she'll just be a rebound girl."

He chuckled. "And that would be a problem because…?"

"You try to sound like such a heartless jerk, but you're actually a good guy."

"And yet you choose him over me."

"I knew him first," she said, shrugging, as if it was as simple as that.

They'd arrived at the stairs to the second floor, and climbed together in silence. When they got to the top, Evan followed Macey to her side of the building. Outside her door, she faced him.

"I had fun tonight," she said.

"Liar."

She flicked him on the upper arm, which was hard as marble. "I did. I know you didn't, though. Sorry about that."

"Nothing to apologize for. I'll see you at the pool in a couple days."

He leaned down and kissed her on the forehead, and for a heartbeat, she wondered if she'd decided too soon she wasn't interested. The notion passed and she was just glad he was understanding. "Definitely. Thanks, Evan."

He squeezed her hand gently before walking off. When he was two doors down, he turned toward her but kept walking backward. "He does have feelings for you, Macey. And if I had to guess, there's nothing brotherly about them at all."

Evan was inside his own apartment before Macey could form a coherent sentence to set him straight.

She allowed herself to imagine, just for a minute, what it would be like if he were somehow right.

CHAPTER ELEVEN

DEREK GOT OUT OF his truck and headed to the locked door of The Shell Shack, dodging the fat raindrops that had just started coming down. Thick clouds covered the sky and the wind was picking up. It was likely to be a slow day for business and that was just fine with him.

He opened one set of wood shutters to let some light in, then dragged out the heavy-duty plastic covers that snapped over the openings on rainy days. If the wind didn't let up, it'd be a bitch to get them attached by himself.

Before he started, he went into the kitchen and got the coffeemaker going. He'd had an extra hard time sleeping last night and would need as much help as possible getting through the wimpy eight-hour shift Macey had scheduled him for. He still wasn't comfortable with not being here every hour the place was open, but he'd run out of arguments and had made her a promise that he'd only work the shifts she scheduled him. He wasn't any better rested than he'd been when working open to close every day.

When he came back out of the kitchen, Gus was seated on his usual stool.

"It's 10:00 a.m.," Derek said. "What are you doing here?"

"It's noon somewhere." His uncle, wearing his usual bucket hat and a gaudy plaid, button-down shirt that tented on his bony body, spread out the newspaper in front of him. "Took the early shuttle today. Got me a date this afternoon."

"You've got a date?" Maybe the sky was actually falling and those weren't just heavy clouds out there.

"Don't act so surprised, boy," Gus said smugly. "I've had plenty of women in my time."

"You haven't had any since I've been here. You've been too busy watching over my shoulder to notice any besides Macey and Andie."

"Thelma lives down the hall at the retirement home. Had my eye on her since she moved in."

"Finally made your big move, huh?"

"We're going to a matinee." Gus's excitement, or maybe it was self-satisfaction, made his eyes shine.

"Well, good for you. One of us should be getting some action."

"Since when are you interested in action, boy?"

"I'm not."

Something about seeing Macey out with what's-his-name had jump-started a part of his brain that had been dead. Specifically the part that was concerned with getting some action. He'd woken up in a sweat—and not a cold one. He'd gotten up, taken an icy shower and gone running, even though it hadn't quite been 5:00 a.m.

"You gonna help me with these things?" he asked

Gus, carrying the plastic sheets to the outer wall where he'd opened the shutters.

"Wasn't planning on it, no."

Derek hoisted himself up on the wooden counter that lined the perimeter of the bar and started snapping the top of the plastic into place. "Too bad. Would've paid you in liquor."

"Like hell you would've. Damn teetotaler," Gus grumbled as he hobbled toward the opposite end of the opening and held the plastic in place.

"If I'm a teetotaler then you're a saint."

"I'll drink to that."

"Not until I get you your drink, you won't," Derek said, moving across to Gus's side and working his way down to the bottom snaps.

"You're awful crotchety today, boy."

"I don't have a date, remember?"

"Maybe you should get one."

"Like hell."

"I suppose you think that wouldn't be proper because of what happened to your girlfriend." Gus's voice went soft, as if he was hesitant to bring up the subject of Julie.

"I suppose you're going to tell me it would be."

"I don't know a damn thing about what's proper or improper, but I do suspect she'd never want you to piss your life away because she died."

"You done yet?" Derek asked, moving to the next set of shutters and unlocking them.

"Eh, I'm not done till I quit drawin' breath."

"That's what I was afraid of."

His uncle had made his slow way over to this opening and continued to help. Derek glanced at him as the older man stretched to reach the top. Gus's arms shook with age and exertion and Derek instantly felt like an asshole.

"I got this," he said. "Go sit down and I'll get you your whiskey as soon as I'm done."

Gus stubbornly continued snapping his side, and Derek shrugged and finished the bottom of the plastic.

A few minutes later, Gus had his drink and Derek was behind the counter slicing lemons.

"Can I ask you something without you biting my head off?" Gus asked.

"I'm not going to bite your head off."

"The way you're going after that fruit…what happened?"

"What do you mean?"

"You're worse than a scorned hormonal woman today. What's going on?"

"Not a thing."

Macey.

It bothered him that she'd gone on a date. Wouldn't have mattered if it was the firefighter or the pope. Seeing her out with someone made Derek want to punch things.

He was in no position to react that way.

He turned to the lemon supply and sliced two of them vigorously, taking pleasure from the sound of the knife smacking the cutting board and echoing through the empty bar.

Ultimately, though, the lemons didn't make him feel much better so he wiped his hands clean and took out two shot glasses. He set them on the counter in front of Gus with a clank, then grabbed the top-shelf tequila and filled them.

"What's this for?" Gus asked.

Derek leveled a look at him. "I don't believe in much anymore, Uncle Gus, but I do believe in the power of tequila."

Gus nodded. "I'll drink to that. Here's to the holy agave. Happy Sunday, boy."

Three shots took the edge off and by the time Macey came in at noon, Derek felt as if he might be able to set aside his feelings about her and her date. In fact, he was determined to.

CHAPTER TWELVE

SOMETHING WAS UP WITH Derek.

He'd worked until six as he'd been scheduled to do, but then instead of leaving, he'd camped out on the end stool with a bottle of top-shelf tequila and a special glass he'd dug out. He explained it was for tequila sipping, which was news to Macey, but then she'd stayed away from tequila ever since one particularly bad night in college.

In all the years she had known Derek, she'd witnessed him drinking alcohol plenty of times, but never with the sole intent to get drunk. Tonight, he was drinking to get drunk. And he was pretty close to it, if not beyond, by the time Macey's shift was over at eight.

"Hey, waste-oid, I'm taking you to dinner so you can sober up," she said after clocking out.

"Don't wanna sober up."

"Tough. You're too old for this kind of crap."

"Not even twenty-nine yet."

"Remind yourself that in the morning when you're paying for it."

Derek laughed sloppily and she should've realized then how far gone he was. But he was sitting up fairly straight and not being obnoxious. He'd actually been pretty quiet, talking to a few people who sat next to him but not getting loud or unruly at all.

Andie was closing with Charlotte, one of their latest hires—a woman in her late fifties with a decided smoker's rasp—so Macey made sure they had everything they needed to get through the last few hours.

"You taking him home?" Andie asked, motioning to where Derek sat.

"Going to get him some food. If that doesn't help, I'll throw him in the shower."

"If you really want to wake him up, jump in with him."

Charlotte laughed huskily. "I like the way this girl thinks."

"I would if I was half as naughty as you two," Macey said. "I'll see you guys later."

"Good luck with Super Drunk," Andie told her.

"Don't let his cute little tush drown in the shower, honey," Charlotte added.

"I don't think he's that bad off. He'll be fine." She picked up her purse and went around the bar to Derek. "Come on."

"Come on, what?"

"We're leaving."

"I'm not done yet."

"Give the bottle to Andie and she'll save it for you for later. I'm taking you to dinner."

"We can eat here."

"I have a gallon of beer spilled on my shirt. We're

going to my place so I can change and then we're going somewhere different."

"You look good the way you are," he said, and she wished he were sober and she really did look good.

"I'm sure I smell nice, too. If you have a thing for breweries."

He leaned into her and sniffed her chest. "Sure do. Fresh hops."

"Derek," she said, trying to scold him. "Let's go. Where are your keys?"

"Keys for what?" He stood but made no move to hand over anything.

Macey took a breath and reached into the front pocket of his shorts. She chuckled when she felt the dolphin she'd added after their cruise.

"Oh, baby," Derek said loudly. "Didn't know you felt that way."

"Get 'im, honey," Charlotte rasped.

Macey removed her hand as quickly as possible, after snagging the keys. She would never have tried that if he was sober, but no way was she letting him drive his truck now.

She also wasn't going to be able to lead him far on foot, she realized as they headed out of The Shell Shack. She'd thought maybe they could walk to her apartment, but he moved slowly, and if she unwound her arm from his, she was pretty sure walking straight would be a chore for him.

Macey unlocked the passenger door of his truck. "Get in."

He did as she said, and she went around to the driver's side.

"Start thinking of a place to go for dinner."

He didn't respond and when she looked over at him, he just smiled at her with a little-boy smile that half melted her heart.

It took her a few seconds to adjust the mirrors and to move the driver's seat forward enough that she could reach the pedals. Thank goodness they weren't going far. This thing was four times the size of her Toyota.

While she parked at her apartment, Derek just sat there. She got out and went around to his side of the truck to open his door. "Come on. It won't take me long to change. You want to jump in the shower first?"

"No." He climbed out and took her hand as they headed for the staircase, as if they were on a date and he were sober enough to lead her anywhere. Instead of worrying about it, she just enjoyed the feel of his large, rough-skinned hand around hers for the few seconds it lasted.

He paused at the bottom of the stairs and she convinced him to go up by promising him he could rest while she got ready.

And that was the last of their conversation.

When Macey returned to the living room after changing, she found him sprawled on the too-short couch. Out cold. She shook her head and couldn't help laughing. Fortunately, he hadn't been an annoying drunk.

She made sure he was breathing, then went out for food. She drove through a fast-food place and got enough for both of them, knowing Derek would be starving when he woke up. To her knowledge, he hadn't had anything to eat since lunch.

Back at her apartment, Macey turned on the television and sat on the floor in front of the couch to eat her burger and fries. He didn't stir.

An hour later, she flipped the TV off. She looked at Derek, who'd barely moved.

"Derek." She sat on the edge of the couch and shook his arm in an attempt to rouse him. Maybe he'd wake up and feel like going out for a couple of hours. "Hey, tequila boy, wake up."

He groaned something she couldn't understand and rolled over onto his side.

"Are you hungry?" she asked, figuring if anything would get him to stir it'd be food. "Come on, Derek. You're wasting the whole night."

He rolled so he was facing her, and opened his eyes. "You're beautiful, Mace."

He pulled her to lie down next to him and she stretched her legs out alongside his. Derek's arm rested on her waist and her heart pounded so loudly she was sure he could hear it. Then…nothing. He drifted back to sleep, breathing heavily and evenly, smelling like a bar.

Macey had dreamed for years of being this close to him, but this wasn't cutting it. Call her picky, but she preferred him to be conscious.

She lifted his arm from her waist before slipping off the couch. "Sleep well, Dare." She kissed his unmoving head and retreated to her room.

It was early still. She could at least salvage the night by getting some work done.

DEREK OPENED HIS EYES reluctantly, wondering what wrecking ball he'd gotten into a fight with. His pulse throbbed in his temples and the base of his skull felt as if it'd been disconnected from the rest of his body. There wasn't a single drop of moisture in his mouth and he had to check to make sure his tongue was still there.

He took note of his surroundings, wondering where the hell he was and how he'd gotten here.

Macey's apartment.

He didn't remember going to Macey's.

Macey's couch. Damned if this wasn't the most uncomfortable damn thing he'd ever slept on in his life. He tried to stretch, but it was a foot too short. He sat up and put his feet on the floor. Every inch of his body ached, some of it post-exercise pain, which he was used to, but some of it post God-knew-what. What the hell had he done?

Tequila. The good stuff. Or bad, depending on your perspective.

He tried to moisten his lips, succeeding only marginally. He needed water. Needed to soak in it for hours. Ah, a glass of water on the end table. She was a goddess. He downed it in seconds.

Derek pushed himself up and headed toward the bathroom—the only one was through Macey's bedroom. Hopefully, she was still asleep and he could sneak in and out….

Oh, sweet God above.

Macey's door was open and she wasn't sleeping. She stood with her back to him, getting dressed. His feet felt mired in glue, and he stared as she pulled her silky sky-blue panties up her legs to cover her perfectly rounded ass. Any moisture he'd summoned into his mouth before was once again gone, and he felt himself harden instantly.

He got an eyeful of her beautiful breasts as she picked up her bra from the dresser. Then she spotted him and crossed her arms over her chest.

"Whoops," he muttered, unable to turn away. He'd apologize, but that view... He wasn't sorry in the least.

MACEY FELT HER BODY HEAT from the inside out as Derek stared at her. And stared. Instead of embarrassment, though, desire pumped through her with every heartbeat. Something about the keen interest in his eyes. The way he *kept* looking at her. The way his Adam's apple seemed to get stuck as he swallowed hard.

He should've turned away and left the room several seconds ago, but he hadn't. Macey brazenly dropped her arms to her sides and gave him something to look at. Derek's eyes met hers, then wandered back down her body, making her heart pound harder from both nervousness and need.

Her brain went on hiatus and she slowly stepped toward him. The idea of his powerful arms around her, now, like this, became all consuming. When she was inches away from him, she stopped and stared up. His eyes met hers and burned a hole through her.

She had to touch him.

Timidly at first, she reached out to his sculpted chest, covered by a T-shirt. He didn't move away, and she couldn't stop herself from stepping even closer to him, running her hands over his pecs, feeling the hard muscle beneath her fingers. She trailed them up and over his shoulders.

Derek still didn't resist. He looked ready to devour her. She could think of nothing but being devoured as she stood on tiptoe and kissed him.

His hands were instantly on her waist and lower, touching her everywhere, pulling her closer still. His unmistakable arousal pressed into her abdomen as he let out a sexy, carnal moan. His tongue swept inside her mouth and they explored each other greedily.

Her breasts pressed against the butter-soft cotton of his T-shirt, but she wanted skin. She ran her hands under the bottom hem of his shirt, raising it in a rush to feel his heat directly on her body. They parted just enough for her to yank the shirt off.

The glance she got at his bare chest would've made her swallow her tongue if it wasn't already occupied with his again. He was so beautiful.... Everything she'd dreamed of and yet so much more than she ever could've imagined. Right here, in her arms. Touching her, wanting her.

Her head swam.

Derek's hands crept beneath her panties and she felt

the roughness of his fingers all over her backside. Her pulse throbbed where her ache was centered.

It occurred to her that Derek wasn't in the right mental state for this, but instead of pulling away, she decided maybe distraction could do something for him. There was no way she could walk away from him now, anyway. She focused all her affection and everything she'd ever felt for him into her kisses and caresses, hoping he could somehow understand how much she cared.

Then she once again lost all coherent thought. This might be the only time she was ever this close to Derek, and she intended to remember every millisecond of it, every inch of him.

His hands slid upward, toward her waist, and she tried not to be disappointed that he'd left her panties on. For now. He worked his way up her sides to her breasts. He palmed them, kneaded them. Teased them until she gasped with the need to have him inside her.

Before she could draw a full breath, his hands had slipped around her torso, away from her breasts. His manner changed; she wasn't sure how, but she sensed it. He wrapped his arms tightly around her and buried his face in her hair, holding her so close that she couldn't see his face, couldn't kiss him. Could only wonder what had changed.

"I can't do this, Mace."

Oh. That.

She'd never needed someone as she did right now. Derek. Only Derek. Now that she'd been this close to him, she didn't know how she could ever settle for another man.

"What's wrong, Dare?" she finally managed to say in a rough, half-there voice, more as a stalling tactic than not knowing what was bothering him. She knew all too well.

He pulled away and peered down at her, but a shutter had closed, blocking her from seeing any real emotions. He was shutting her out once again, just like that.

"I'm gonna take a shower and get out of here. I'm sorry, Macey."

Sorry. That was the last thing she ever wanted to hear after a scene like that. She should be the one to apologize, but couldn't bring herself to say a word. Instead, she raised her chin a notch, nodded and turned away from him, as if she was going to get dressed and go on with her life.

As if.

CHAPTER THIRTEEN

FOR ONCE MACEY COULDN'T focus on her nonprofit project, even though she had the entire day off from the bar. She couldn't stop thinking about Derek.

She grabbed her keys from the kitchen counter and headed outside. A walk along the shore was in order. The wide-open space and the sounds of the water tended to clear her head and help her put things in perspective.

She was walking between two resort hotels to get to the beach when she felt something damp on the back of her calf. She looked down and saw a shaggy black-and-white dog, a puppy, really, playing tag with her flip-flop.

"Hey, pooch, what are you doing?" She put her hand out and he licked it eagerly, making her laugh. "Where's your home?"

He looked up at her with big puppy-dog eyes and she could swear the dog was sad. Or hungry. Maybe both. She could see every one of his ribs and there was no spare meat on his tummy. "You hungry? I don't have anything for you."

He walked alongside her, tail wagging.

"You need to go home and get some dinner."

The dog did no such thing, though. He stayed close

to her and matched her pace as she angled north. She kind of enjoyed the comfortable companionship, but soon found her thoughts heading right back to Derek.

He'd taken off that morning as soon as he'd finished showering, even though she'd offered him breakfast—never mind that it wasn't a nutritionally sound breakfast. It was better than what he normally ate, which consisted of coffee and little else, she would bet.

He hadn't had to be at work for another two hours, but he'd run off, anyway. Undoubtedly because of what had happened between them.

Remembering how her body had reacted to him when it wasn't supposed to, even before they'd touched, her face heated. Her intention had been to be the friend he needed. She'd never acted so boldly and would never, ever have the guts to do so again. Not after his rejection.

So back to being friends and friends only, regardless of their intimacy this morning. She'd given him the chance to distract himself from his problems, and he'd refused. She would have to find another way to help him. Back to the original plan, whatever that was.

She'd failed so far in getting him to open up, to talk through some of his grief. Nothing had changed for him since she'd been here. He still wasn't doing anything but working and exercising compulsively. Brooding. Being antisocial.

Getting drunk off his butt.

She was down to just a couple of weeks left on the island before she planned to head back to Dallas and really dig in to her project. She hated to face Derek's mom and tell her she'd been right. Macey hadn't been able to help him.

Which left her with a lot of work to do in a short time.

Before she realized it, she was walking past The Shell Shack. Derek was working, she knew, so she avoided going in. She wasn't ready to face him, but she would get over that soon, figure out how to salvage her trip and somehow get through to him.

Though she stayed far enough away from the bar that no one inside would spot her, that didn't stop her from straining to see what Derek was doing. As usual, her heart skipped at the sight of him. She wondered if that reaction would ever stop.

The dog nuzzled her hand as if to remind her she should keep moving, and she reached down to pet him. "We need to find out if you have a home," she said. She turned around and headed back toward her apartment, and the dog stuck to her side as if they'd walked the beach together for years.

"You're an awesome dog, aren't you?" He licked her hand again. "You'd be good for Derek," she said thoughtfully. Maybe a pet would bring him out of himself, make him think about something besides the fire that had killed Julie.

It was worth a shot, whether this dog was available or not. Macey decided she'd hang some fliers to locate the pup's owner, and if she hadn't heard in a few days, she'd set him up with a brand-new owner. Though Derek wouldn't in a million years admit it, the two of them, pooch and man, needed each other. If she couldn't make him come round, maybe someone of the canine persuasion could.

THREE DAYS HAD PASSED since Derek had played the idiot by not doing an immediate U-turn out of Macey's room Monday morning. Three never-ending days full of fighting off the memory of her silky, baby-soft skin, her hint-of-lilac scent, her curves filling his hands and fitting against his body so perfectly.

Working with her, being on the same island as her, made it all the more difficult. Yesterday they'd shared an eight-hour shift and Derek had remained semi-aroused the entire time. There was no amount of frigid water that could dull the ache.

He glanced over at Macey now as she smiled at a group of customers and handed out their drink order. If The Shell Shack survived, she'd be the reason. She was a natural. Just what the bar needed, but the last thing *he* needed. If he hadn't made a promise to Gus, Derek would be damn tempted just to walk away from it, before he did something stupid.

Like touch Macey again.

As Derek delivered a burger and fries to someone at the outer counter, his uncle appeared in the doorway on the beach side. He shuffled over to his usual place and situated himself on the stool.

Derek made his way back behind the bar. "I was starting to think you'd turned up your toes," he said.

"No sirree," Gus said heartily. "Sorry to disappoint."

Derek set a full glass of whiskey in front of him. "Don't go putting words in my mouth. Somehow this place survived for three days without you, though."

Gus nodded but didn't say anything. The look on his face was pure cat-ate-the-canary, and Derek wondered what'd gotten into the old man.

"You're gonna make me ask, aren't you?" Derek refilled his own soft drink, feeling parched after serving the lunch crowd, which had just cleared out fifteen minutes before.

"Ask what?"

"Where've you been? Not like you to miss three days of riding my ass."

"You missed me." His uncle almost seemed to glow.

"Terribly. If you hadn't showed up today I was going to drive to the home to see what the heck happened to you."

"Love happened to me, boy."

Derek raised his eyebrows skeptically and leaned his elbows on the bar, glad for the break in customers. He couldn't help noticing when Macey went outside to wipe down tables. He had to tear his eyes away from the subtle sway of her hips as she walked.

"Thelma is making me a happy man."

"Glad to hear it. You could've brought her around to the bar, you know."

"Could've. Didn't. You don't need me, anyway. This place doesn't need me."

Derek studied Gus. "This is your life, man. Has been for as long as I can remember. What gives? You dumping us?"

Gus took a sip of whiskey and shook his head slowly. "It's time for me to move on. Not from you, of course, but from this old girl." He patted the counter. "You and your woman there…" He gestured toward Macey, who was wiping off the counter around the outside of the bar now. "You've got it under control. I'm okay with moving on."

Derek straightened and tapped the wood surface several times, deciding to ignore the part about "his woman." It was true that with Macey there they really didn't need Gus's guidance. Hopefully the momentum would carry on when she left, too. What he questioned, though, was whether his uncle would be okay without the bar. "I wish you the best with Thelma. I'd still like to meet her."

"You will, boy. Maybe we'll all go to a fancy dinner."

"Maybe we will."

Macey came back around to Derek's side of the bar and bent over to wring out her towel. Dammit. When she looked like that, wearing short shorts that hugged her bottom perfectly, he had no prayer of *not* remembering the way her body had felt the other day in her bedroom.

Gus chuckled. "So that's how it is then."

Derek looked at him. "What's how it is?" Surely Gus wouldn't open his big mouth with Macey so close.

He simply nodded, glanced at Macey and back at Derek, and grinned like the ornery old fart he was. "I'm on to you, boy."

"Nothing to be on to."

Derek might be obsessed with Macey's body—and what red-blooded male wouldn't be?—but he wouldn't allow himself to feel anything beyond friendship and maybe a touch of ill-advised lust here and there.

It was harder to recall the image of Julie now, but he did. Forced it. He needed to. Needed to remind himself that the woman he'd cared about enough to marry was dead, and he was in no position to think of anyone else.

CHAPTER FOURTEEN

"YOU ARE GOING TO LOSE ME my happy home."

Macey tossed another dog biscuit to the pup, who she'd started calling Burnaby. Unwise, she knew, because she was getting attached. If someone called to claim him…

But no one had. She'd plastered fliers everywhere and had yet to receive a call.

Today was her day off and Derek worked until six. Then, unbeknownst to him, he was going to become a puppy papa, like it or not. Macey was hedging her bets on "not."

But she had faith. Burnaby would win him over. He had to, because Macey was not supposed to have animals in her apartment and she'd almost gotten caught by the landlord twice. Evan and Clay had helped her out of one jam by playing along with her story that she was a dog-sitter and had come home because of an emergency. They'd let the dog out periodically while she was at work as well, on the days they weren't at the station.

"Twenty more minutes and you get to meet your new master."

She was uneasy at the thought of going to Derek's. They hadn't been together outside of work since Monday morning, and of course hadn't discussed their Big Mistake.

She had to refer to it that way in her mind, even though, if given the chance, she wouldn't take back anything she'd done. The only thing she'd change if she could was the last bit. She wanted her happy ending, even though it wasn't going to happen. Having a taste of Derek was just enough to torture her and make her want more.

"Let's take a walk on the beach, Burn."

The dog hurried over to her, tail wagging, as if he could understand. More likely he noticed the leash and knew that meant a walk. He was a smart pup and she would love to keep him if she had a place for him. But she'd be staying with her mom in Dallas to save money, and her mom didn't do dogs. She was allergic, so Macey had never been able to have a pet.

She bent down and attached the leash to his collar, then made a final stop at the mirror to make sure she looked okay. If pressed, she'd have to admit she'd spent too much time selecting her outfit—a denim miniskirt and a feminine, peach-colored cami with lace trim. Casual enough, she hoped, to pass for "just walking on the beach." Her hair fell down her back, slightly messy, but it'd only get worse outside. Her cheeks had a tinge of pink from her lying out in the sun today, and she'd put minimal eye makeup on. She applied clear lip gloss, then slipped on her silver-beaded flip-flops. "Let's go, puppy. Off to your new home."

The dog looked up at her with those eager eyes and she

hoped like crazy Derek was as affected by them as she was. If he refused to keep the dog, she had no idea what she'd do. She hadn't dared to think about that, because frankly, this was her last idea for helping Derek, and her only idea for helping the dog.

Burnaby led her along at a good pace, as if he knew he had an important date. Before hitting the beach, they stopped at the island grocery store and bought steaks, potatoes, dog food, strawberry cheesecake and a few seasonings and kitchen items Derek wouldn't have. Burnaby was hard to resist, but food should at least get them in the door if the dog didn't melt his heart instantly. That would give Macey the opportunity to persuade Derek he needed a pet.

It was almost seven when Macey and Burnaby arrived at Derek's condo. Her nerves were strung tight for too many reasons to count, but she led the dog around to the door on the street side and knocked. He'd presumably left it unlocked, as usual, but she wasn't about to barge in with a dog.

"Hey," Derek said when he opened the door. His hair was wet, as if he'd just showered. He wore a pair of old cargo shorts and held a white T-shirt in his hand. "What the…"

"Hi." Macey attempted a relaxed smile, but he didn't notice anything but the dog. "This is Burnaby."

"Okay. Why is Burnaby here?"

"We brought dinner."

His attention switched to the grocery bag in her left hand.

"Better. What'd you bring? I don't smell any take-out."

"That's because we're cooking it ourselves. Don't look at me that way." She walked past him with the dog, hurrying to the kitchen to set the bag down and give her aching arms a break.

"Macey, what's up with the canine?" Derek called after her as she reached the counter.

"The *canine* has been my houseguest for a few days."

"You can't have dogs."

"Yep. Didn't you see the fliers?"

"What fliers?"

Best not to reveal her cards yet, she figured, and didn't answer.

He joined her at the counter and began unloading the grocery bag. His hands caught her attention and she let herself remember the way they had scorched her bare skin in places few men had ever touched. She shook her head and busied herself going through his kitchen drawers and cabinets. "Where are your pans?"

"What pans?"

"Any pans. Something to use in the oven?"

"What oven?"

"This—" Macey looked at him and realized he was now giving her a hard time. "Pathetic bachelor. Forget the pans. Does your grill work?"

"What grill?"

She punched him lightly, deciding as she made contact

that touching him in any way was a stupid idea. Then she saw that this time he was being serious.

"The grill. On your patio." She walked toward the sliding door and nodded when she spotted it. "I take it you don't know if it works."

"You take it correctly. Never noticed it."

"What do you eat?"

"Burgers. Shrimp. Whatever I pick up at the bar. What am I supposed to eat?"

"You're having steak tonight if you can fire that baby up."

Burnaby, whose leash she'd let go of, shook himself at that moment and scratched, drawing Derek's attention back to him.

"What's the dog eating?"

"You could share your steak with him."

"Don't hold your breath."

"You starting that grill yet?"

"I'll take a look at it."

"Looking won't cook your dinner."

"Mace, that thing's ancient. I'm not in the mood to have your firefighter buddies here on business."

She rolled her eyes. Ever the firefighter, alert to dangers. Just proved he needed to get back to the career he'd been born to do.

He opened the door and Burnaby made a rush for it. Derek grabbed for him and Macey hollered the dog's name—the one he didn't recognize as his yet—but both were futile. Burnaby was on the loose.

"He likes the beach," Macey explained, hurrying past Derek. "Come on. We need to catch him."

Derek ambled outside, his hands in the pockets of his shorts. "You're kidding."

"Do I look like I'm kidding?" she called back to him. "Go get the dog treats out of the sack. Burnaby! Come here, boy!"

Seconds later, Derek joined her, opening the package of bone-shaped biscuits. Macey whistled and Burnaby paused to look at her, then took off in a wild semicircle.

"That dog needs some discipline," Derek said as he slowly approached.

"A little puppy training and some love and attention from you will do the trick."

Derek peered suspiciously at her then. "No. No way. No, no and more no, Macey. I'm not taking the dog."

Oops. That wasn't how she'd hoped to bring up the subject. "He's a good dog, Derek. Except when let loose on the beach. Burnaby, come here!"

This was a giant game for the puppy, who sprinted toward the water, away from Macey, then froze, snowy ears at attention, and changed direction. She made another run for him, hoping to catch up with him and grab his collar, but he had other ideas.

It didn't take long for her to get completely winded and frustrated. She bent over, bracing her weight on her knees, gasping for air.

In the distance, Derek squatted down, crinkled the

plastic of the treat package and spoke in a normal voice to Burnaby. Ha. As if that would...

The traitor trotted over to Derek, stumpy little tail wagging, and gobbled the treat from his hand. Derek took hold of his collar as he knelt next to Burnaby, who promptly licked his face. Macey couldn't help laughing.

"Your dog seriously lacks manners," Derek called.

"Not my dog. He's yours."

"I don't want a dog."

"He wants you."

Burnaby was going after the bag that Derek now held over his head. His tail whipped back and forth and he jumped up on Derek's leg.

"Patience, mutt. I'll give you another treat. *One.* First you have to go back inside."

Macey jogged up to them. "See? You're a natural."

"Not taking the dog."

She didn't speak until they were safely inside with the door closed again. "I don't know what else to do with him," she finally said quietly. "I can't keep him."

"You'll only be in your apartment for a little longer. You can take him with you."

"Not to my mom's."

He nodded, as if now remembering the whole allergy thing. "I'll check out the grill if you hold the monster back."

She called the dog and offered him one more treat when he finally sat in front of her. "Good puppy."

Derek slipped outside, shutting the door quickly.

"Derek's nicer than he seems," she told the dog. "Just wait. He'll fall in love with you and give you lots of dog biscuits."

Burnaby's tail sped up again like a pendulum on speed.

"Hope you have a plan B," Derek said as he came back in. "That grill is a serious fire hazard. I need to trash it completely."

She knew better than to argue. Instead she headed back to the kitchen and pulled out the foil she'd brought. "I'll figure something out." The meat would eventually cook, she hoped. Potatoes, too. "We could have dessert first."

The glimmer that flashed in his eyes made her realize her mistake in word choice. "I mean...I brought strawberry cheesecake. It's ready to go. The main course might take a while."

"I can wait for the meat."

She cut her brain off from any puns that brought to mind. "You wouldn't make me let Burnaby go, would you? The shelter's overcrowded and he wouldn't stand a chance."

"Mace, I'm barely able to take care of myself. How do you think I'm going to do with a mutt depending on me?"

"Step up to the challenge? Maybe be drawn out of this...nonexistence you've created for yourself?"

"My 'nonexistence' suits me just fine, thanks."

She had the meat spread out on the broiler pan she'd finally located in the oven drawer, and was sprinkling seasonings on it. "Slice these up for us, please?" She set the potatoes she'd just washed in front of him. "You can look at keeping Burnaby as a favor to me, then, if that makes it more appealing."

"I'm not in favor mode. I'm sorry, Macey. You of all people know that."

"Look at that dog's eyes and tell me you can force him out on the street."

He seemed about to argue some more but then paused as if listening to something. Macey automatically glanced at Burnaby to make sure he wasn't chewing on the furniture, as he was wont to do. The romp on the beach must've worn him out, though; he was sprawled on the beat-up couch, sound asleep.

She realized what Derek heard just as he made his way down the hall and opened the door onto the street. The siren of a fire truck blared in the distance, growing louder as it neared. It sounded as if it was coming directly down their street. Macey walked up behind Derek to watch. He didn't even notice her—he was intent on the big red rig passing by.

She studied his face instead of the truck, and for a split second saw more than he would ever want her to see, she was sure. *Longing.*

She tried to find something to say but was at a loss. Didn't want to screw it up. This was too important. Instead, she returned to the kitchen and gave him some space. She heard the door shut softly and could tell by the silence that he'd gone outside. She wondered if he was going to follow the truck. At least he'd remembered his new escape-artist roommate and hadn't left the door wide open.

Less than five minutes had passed when he came back inside. He took his place next to Macey and started methodically slicing the potatoes, the click of the knife on the cutting board emphasizing the lack of conversation.

"You can't avoid it forever, Dare," she finally said after sticking the meat in the oven.

"The dog? Pushing me isn't going to—"

"Not the dog." She hoisted herself up onto the counter next to him. "The fire."

There went that shutter over his expression. It was subtle and yet so very plain to see that she wanted to shake him.

"If you'd talk to me about it, maybe I'd leave you alone."

"Don't want to talk about it."

"It doesn't take a shrink to see you're all kinds of messed up. Understandably. I want to help you, Derek, in some little way. Any way."

He kept cutting, not looking at her, not speaking, just slicing away in a slightly freaky even rhythm. Then he set the knife down on the counter, ran both hands over his face and walked away.

Fantastic.

Now what?

She followed him into the spare bedroom-turned-workout room, where he was already lying down to bench some weights. She parked herself on a still-packed moving box against the wall and watched him do seven, eight, nine reps. He kept going and she counted silently, waiting. For what, she wasn't sure. He wouldn't speak, and she wasn't sure what to say, but she was not going to let this pass by. She'd been careful—respectful—since she'd arrived on the island, and it was time to push. She crossed her legs at the ankles and leaned on the wall, watching his biceps flex underneath the sleeves of his Underdog T-shirt, fighting to remain indifferent to that body.

At twenty reps, he stopped and lay there, catching his breath. He stared at the ceiling as she stared at him, wishing she could will him to speak.

"You want to go back, don't you? To firefighting?" she said quietly into the heavy silence.

He hesitated. Shook his head minutely. "Can't do it."

"I get that. You've said that. What I asked was if you *want* to. I saw it on your face when the truck went by, Derek."

"What I'm trying to tell *you,* and you're refusing to hear, is that it doesn't matter if I have a random urge to go back to it. God, if I could go back to a year ago, I would in a heartbeat."

"Yeah. I know some of what that feels like. Experienced it when my dad died. Again when my mom was so sick. It sucks."

She wasn't sure what she expected, but it wasn't what she got. He shook his head again, subtly at first, then he sat up and shook it with so much conviction she straightened, alarmed.

"No. You can't know what it feels like. You can't begin to imagine how it is to be responsible for the death of someone you were supposed to love."

Macey's mouth gaped open. "I—"

"Don't. Don't try to tell me you have any idea what it's like."

He was blaming himself for not saving Julie and Billy. Un-be-lievable.

Or maybe not.

As the seconds ticked by and Macey thought about it, it wasn't such a shock, after all. She was an idiot not to suspect it or consider it before now. He'd worked the fire. Julie and Billy had died. He'd been right there and not been able to do anything to help them.

Why hadn't Macey seen it? She closed her eyes against tears.

"The building collapsed, Derek." One of the few details from the fire that she knew. She swallowed. "That happens during fires."

Derek got up and walked out of the room.

She sat there for a good ten minutes, wondering how in the world to make him see this objectively. It wouldn't get rid of his grief—nothing ever would—but alleviating his unwarranted guilt could only be a positive step.

The shower in the master bedroom turned on. She rushed out, remembering the steaks were still in the oven. Ready to be turned over, at the very least. Maybe charred beyond recognition. She had no earthly idea how much time had passed while they were in the other room.

They were salvageable, whether she and Derek would have appetites or not. Macey flipped them over and distractedly added the pan of potatoes to the upper rack of the oven.

When Derek walked into the kitchen a few minutes later, Macey watched from the couch, sitting next to Burnaby, who hadn't stirred. Derek surprised her by coming all the way into the living room and sitting down on the floor. He leaned against the couch in front of the dog, propped his elbows on his knees and covered his eyes with his palms.

She took it as a good sign that she hadn't had to chase him down. It was all she could do, though, to wait for him to say something. *He* had to begin. She stroked Burnaby's fur over and over to distract herself from all the questions she wanted to ask, the things she was dying to say. Finally, Derek uncovered his face and stared straight ahead.

"It was a four-alarm fire. We were the second team in. Julie wasn't supposed to be working that day, so when I realized the shop she worked in was involved, I kept it together, thanking God she was with her family and nowhere near the fire." His voice was gravelly, full of raw emotion.

"The fire had started in the shop next to hers, so we were sent in there to help Engine 17 put it out. We ran a dry two-and-a-half hose line up there because there was so much fire and smoke showing. I was on the nozzle.

Place was so full of smoke we couldn't see a thing, but we made our way to the second floor."

He exhaled hard, as if this was taking a toll on him physically, then ran his hands through his hair.

"We'd no sooner gotten into position than flames started to roll across the ceiling. Aaron Maloney was with me, hauling hose. I radioed the pump operator to charge the line with water, and then the next second the whole thing flashed over."

Macey's pulse raced as she imagined Derek in such danger. He'd explained to her in the past that sometimes the rapid buildup of heat in a fire caused everything combustible in a room to spontaneously ignite, spreading the fire instantly—a flashover—often trapping the firefighters inside a room entirely filled with flames.

"We had to get the hell out of there. The flames made it brighter than the sun and just as hot, but the smoke was so thick it was still nearly impossible to see our way. We followed the hose line to the staircase we'd come up, and dived down it. It all happened within seconds."

"You dived down stairs?" Macey asked, her heart pounding.

"We had no choice. Aaron took a pretty hard fall, cracked some ribs and broke his arm, but he softened my landing. The fire seemed to follow us down and I lugged him along, trying to find a back exit, because the entire front of the building seemed to be involved now."

Macey crept onto the floor next to him, folded her legs beneath her and propped one arm on the couch so she faced Derek's side. He didn't move or appear to notice that she had.

"Never did find a back door, so I passed him out a window to a bystander and climbed out after him. Carrying him caused him excruciating pain, so I left him with the civilian and went to find a way around to the front to get an EMT there. I'd lost my portable radio inside."

Burnaby stood and shook, making his collar jingle. He turned around on the couch a couple times, lay back down, and Derek continued.

"Those buildings were built about three feet apart, which is why the fire consumed so many of them. It just jumped from one to the next. I had to run up to the end of the block to get around. I didn't know it then but they'd called in two more companies after mine. At that point, my first concern was for Aaron, getting him some help."

"The EMTs were all on the other side?"

Derek nodded absently. "We'd been told when we arrived that most of the businesses were closed on Sunday. No one was aware of anyone inside. Residents of the top floor of the building to the north had been the ones to call in the alarm, and had gotten out safely long ago. The other buildings didn't have residential units. All commercial.

"While I'd been inside, though, the initial report had changed. There were two cars in the parking lot, in spaces employees of the different businesses usually used. They'd sent some guys in to search the buildings that hadn't been burning when we'd arrived."

His face tightened and she saw him swallow hard. Macey sat up straighter.

"When I got around to the battalion chief in charge, I could see the fire had jumped south to Julie's building and the one next to it. I heard about the two cars, and when they said one was a silver Camry my knees nearly buckled."

"Julie's?" Macey asked quietly, knowing the answer from Derek's agony.

"Chief Valencia had Billy on the radio. He and Carlos had found two people in the basement of Julie's shop. Both blonde females, both unconscious. Carlos had just taken one out a back window—apparently flames blocked the way to the door—and Billy was carrying the other woman, a few feet behind Carlos. I took off running, trying to find a shortcut to them, as soon as I heard."

He leaned his head back on the couch, so he stared at the ceiling—or would have, if his eyes had been open. Macey could tell he was struggling to keep his composure. Grief pulled at his features and she wondered if he was even breathing.

She reached out to him but stopped short, her hand hovering above his arm as she hesitated. She drew it back without making contact, and waited for him to continue with the most horrible part.

CHAPTER FIFTEEN

"SIXTY MORE SECONDS and they could've made it," Derek said, his voice gruff with sadness. "Carlos got the other woman out. I'd had to go around the long way to get back there and try to help. I was twenty yards away when the building went down. Just collapsed, both the main and second stories falling into the basement before my eyes."

Macey squeezed his forearm, then took his hand in hers. He surprised her by tightening his grasp instead of pulling away.

"It took forever to reach them. First we had to get the fire under control, then dig through feet of debris. Chief Valencia tried to make me leave several times. Did everything short of shoving me in the truck and driving me away himself. But I couldn't leave her, even once hope for their survival was gone. There was no way they could've made it. No pockets of air, no way they hadn't been crushed under the weight of the two stories."

Macey scooted closer and rested her head on his shoulder, her chest tight.

The timer on the ancient oven started beeping, the tinny, shrill sound dragging her back to the present moment. She couldn't imagine eating now. "Be back in a sec."

She got up and methodically, numbly pulled the steak and potatoes out, paying no heed to whether they were done or not. Tears blinded her and she couldn't care less about the state of the food. After twisting the oven dial to Off, she rejoined Derek, who hadn't moved a muscle.

She didn't hesitate to slide right up next to him and weave their hands together again. He didn't acknowledge her, but that was okay. Minutes passed without them speaking.

"Dare?" she finally said softly. "How do you think you could've stopped the building from falling on them?"

He stared straight ahead, dully, almost catatonically.

"I mean it," she continued. "Firefighters are some of the biggest, bravest heroes out there. You run into burning buildings while everyone else is running out. You save lives, save property…. But you're not God. You can't stop a building from falling down after fire has ripped through it. Can you?"

She saw him struggle to swallow again. His eyes darted around the room, still avoiding her.

"Derek? You can't. Admit that."

His eyes shut and he shook his head.

"So then her death couldn't be your fault. It was just horrible, awful luck that she and Billy were in that basement."

He didn't hesitate in his answer, as if he'd already asked himself this question and had formulated the answer in great detail. "If I'd figured out what was happening just feet away from me—literally maybe fifty feet—when I hauled Aaron out of the first building, I could've gotten in there to her. Could've got her out before the building came down. Maybe even before she lost consciousness."

"You were getting help for Aaron."

"I should've known. You always have to expect the unexpected when you're working a fire. That's rule number one. I could've guessed the fire would move south."

"You'd been told there were no people inside. You were saving the one person you knew had been injured. What could you have done, ignore Aaron and run off on the slim chance your info had been wrong? That's not even logical."

"I failed her. That's all there is to it."

"It's not." Macey kept her voice down when she wanted to scream at him. "I don't care how good you are at your job, Dare. You're still just one man. One man who made the best decisions you could based on the information you'd been given. Until you develop some kind of superpowers, I'm pretty sure that's all anyone can ask of themselves."

"That's not enough."

"It has to be. There was nothing else you could've done. Derek, you loved her. If you could have done *anything* else, you would have. I know that as sure as I need to take my next breath."

He lowered his head to his hands, defeated. Tired and hopeless.

Darkness had fallen at some point and the only illumination came from a security light outside that shone in through the side window. The air conditioner was running and the usual din of the waves seemed a distant, vague sound in the closed-up condo.

Macey stood slowly, feeling as if she'd been dragged along a bumpy track by a freight train. She stretched to get some blood flowing. Burnaby stirred again, jumping down to sit at her feet, tail wagging.

"I need to take him out. Want to come with?" she asked.

Derek shook his head.

"I'll make it quick."

"Take your time. You can't fix my problems, Mace."

She knew that, but she *could* be there with him, and that was something.

The leash was still attached to Burn's collar so she picked it up and followed the excited dog to the door. She held on tightly as she opened it, inhaling the fresh sea air as they stepped outside.

Burnaby did his duty quickly, then wanted to run. Macey was barefoot so she kept to the softer dry sand and jogged along with the dog for a short distance up the beach. The temperature had dropped about twenty degrees since the heat of the day and actually felt good. Almost cool. The exhilaration from running with Burnaby gave Macey a second wind to go back in to Derek and do what, if anything, she could for him.

She took a reluctant dog inside with her and turned

on the dim light over the stove to search for the mini bag of dog food she'd brought. She found two old bowls—actually, all of them were ancient—in the cabinet and put down food and water for Burnaby. Derek still sat in the same place in the living room and didn't say a word. His eyes were closed but she didn't think he was asleep. He looked too stiff and uncomfortable to have drifted off.

She put the steaks and potatoes in the refrigerator for tomorrow and gathered a couple of pillows and blankets from the bedroom. On the way back to the living room, she turned out the stove light. Burnaby was still going at his dinner, famished from all the exercise he'd gotten. Macey dropped the pile of bedding on the floor near Derek.

"What are you doing?" he asked, coming out of his trance.

She went back to the sliding door, opened the glass part and closed the screen, testing it to make sure it would stand up to a determined dog. She left the glass panel open about half a foot—just enough to let in the fresh night air and the meditative sound of the waves.

She spread Derek's comforter on the floor. "Might as well get comfortable," she told him, adjusting a pillow at one end of the makeshift bed. The other she put on the couch, along with the second blanket. "You can stretch out up here."

"That couch isn't suitable for sleeping or even not sleeping. Got more lumps than the Rocky Mountains."

"Then lie on the floor," Macey said, taking the couch herself. It was about ten o'clock, and she was beat.

Derek did stretch out on the floor, on his back, but even in the dim light she could tell he wasn't going to let himself wind down. "Why don't you go home?" he asked her after a few minutes of tense silence. "I don't need a babysitter."

"Sorry. Not leaving you right now. Besides, I'm too tired to move. You'll just have to deal with me."

She tried to get comfortable, but no matter which way she turned, one of the couch's lumps pressed stubbornly into a tender part of her body. After a few more minutes, she sat up. "Move over."

Derek obeyed, proof of how out of sorts he was, since he'd never really been the obeying type. She considered ordering him to roll over and let her massage him again, but she flashed back to the last time she'd tried that, and decided touching him so much wouldn't be wise. Not as run-down and exhausted as they both were. She wouldn't have much willpower to keep it friendly, and it was risky enough to settle just a foot away from him.

She couldn't concentrate on her own feelings right now, or her wishes and desires that always seemed to include this man lying so close to her. Tonight was all about Derek and doing what he needed, *being* what he needed. If that was someone who was just close to him, who kept quiet, then that's what she'd be.

They both lay there without talking for a long time. She wondered if he'd fallen asleep, but there was no even, relaxed breathing. She flipped onto her side, hoping to get more comfortable. The floor wasn't much better than the wretched couch of lumps.

"You still awake?" Derek whispered.

"Yeah. What's up?"

He turned on his side toward her and Macey wrapped her blanket snugly around herself, arms tucked in, for protection—from him, sure, but also from herself.

"What bothers me the most is imagining what must've gone through her mind before she died," he said after another few minutes of silence. "She knew I was on duty that day. I wonder if she was waiting for me to get there, for one of us to save her. I wonder if there was ever…a moment, a thought that flashed through her mind, where she realized I'd let her down."

That was it. Macey's defenses went down and she threw her arms around him. "Oh, jeez, Derek. No. She never thought that. You absolutely didn't let her down."

He wrapped his arm around Macey and held on.

DEREK WOKE UP just before dawn, judging by the bluish-gray tint of the sky. Macey was curled up against him, her back to him, and his arm was still around her. That he hadn't slept this well, this contentedly, in ages should be good news, but it worried him before he was awake enough to figure out why.

His first fully coherent thought was completely inappropriate and made him harder than hell. He realized he was pressed firmly against Macey's soft, perfect ass. Scratch that part about contentment—holding her all night was hell. Waking up so close to her, torture.

He carefully unwound himself, attempting not to wake her up. He needed to get far away fast, before he did something he would regret.

That he could even think of sex was actually big news. The past week or two was the first time there'd been any sign of life below his belt since the fire. He'd wondered if he'd gone half-dead himself. Maybe one of these days he'd do something about his physical needs, but not with Macey. She wasn't a one-night-stand kind of girl, and that's all he'd be able to manage. There was no way he was going to involve himself in anything that required emotions or follow-up.

He tried to roll away but was stopped by a weight against his legs. What the...? The "weight" shook as it scratched itself, and Derek shooed Burnaby out of the way as quietly as possible. When he stood, the dog stood. Oh, happy day, the pup likely needed to go outside to take a leak.

Derek stretched his arms over his head, again wondering at how soundly he'd slept. He had a sneaking suspicion that the cause still lay there slumbering, oblivious.

Oblivious was good.

There was no way to deny that he was attracted to Macey. Ever since she'd been back from Asia, he'd seen her in a different light. She'd blossomed from being like a little sister into a very sexy woman he couldn't ignore.

But he had every intention of trying.

He made his way to the partially open sliding-glass door and was about to hit his thigh to summon the dog, but there was no need. Burnaby galloped over to him, tail going ninety miles an hour. Derek wished he could get so excited about *anything.*

Macey had tossed the leash by the door, so he bent down and fastened it to the dog's collar.

Burnaby surged forward as soon as the screen door was open, and Derek held tightly to his leash. Someone needed to teach this dog who was in charge.

They were soon heading north on the beach, the dog trying to be in the lead until he'd find something—various somethings—interesting enough to sniff at.

"You need obedience school, dog."

That caused another couple wags of the tail and Derek's lips curved upward in spite of himself. He reached down and scratched Burnaby's head.

They spent a few more minutes with the dog raring to go and Derek trying to hold him back before he decided what the heck.

"You wanna run, boy? We'll run."

He started jogging and Burnaby barked once. They picked it up into a near sprint and went for several minutes, pounding the sand side by side.

By the time they stopped, they were at the edge of the developed part of the beach. Walking another quarter of a mile put them technically out of the city limits and into a coastal area protected from development, covered by windswept dunes and patches of sea grass. Broad bands of pinks and oranges spread across the dawn sky and the untouched shore stretched out for miles ahead of them.

Never-ending waves and an invigorating breeze were their only companions out here.

Derek had never ventured up this far. The only place he went besides the bar was his running route, a circuit of a few blocks. Same every time. He'd been missing out.

He and Burnaby settled on top of one of the dunes and stared out at the peaceful gulf, both breathing heavily. Derek let go of the leash and the dog remained by his side in comfortable companionship.

Derek wouldn't have appreciated the scenery before now, he suspected. Something was different today. If he'd known sleeping on the floor was the answer, he would've crawled out of his chair long ago. Too bad the floor wasn't the real reason for his rested state.

It could only be Macey. He would never admit it to her, but voicing what had happened during the fire had caused a strange kind of cathartic release, painful as it had been. Before last night he'd never told a soul what had happened.

Yeah, talking had been important, but even more so was Macey. She was so unselfish. So damn caring by nature. He didn't deserve anything from her and could only hope to someday, somehow repay her for everything she did for him.

He cared about her. Too much. She'd definitely changed in Asia, grown up inside and out. Since she'd been on the island, he'd been drawn to her physically. She was alluring enough that even in his grief and guilt he couldn't help but take notice. It seemed the attraction wasn't entirely one-sided, either, based on the two times they'd kissed. But that was as far as it could go. He was too afraid of hurting her, even if these had been normal times and he wasn't consumed by the tragedy of losing Julie. Macey deserved a good man, and that wasn't him. Not anymore.

He lay back on the sand, supporting his head with his arms, and took in the lightening sky and the splotches of cumulus clouds floating overhead.

Macey was right about one thing. It was time to start finding his way back to life. He needed to do it on his own and leave her out of it, though.

Burnaby sighed and lowered his chin to Derek's thigh.

"You and I just might do all right together, dog."

CHAPTER SIXTEEN

MACEY OPENED ONE EYE to remind herself where she was, as had become a habit. The mustard-yellow couch of lumps loomed over her and it all came back. Derek finally opening up, trusting her enough to talk about Julie and the fire. Sleeping with his arm around her, nestling against her all night. She shivered in contentment and satisfaction, smiling even though she was still half out of it.

At long last they'd made some progress. Mere weeks ago she couldn't even get him to agree to let her stay in the same condo as him, and last night he'd slept with her all night. On the floor. She rubbed her tender left shoulder. Comfort certainly hadn't been what had kept him here.

In her not-quite-awake state, she allowed herself to imagine there was something more between them.

She'd been hyperaware throughout the night of his arm draped over her. The heat of him along her back. Just…him. So close to her.

As she became more alert, the stillness of the condo registered in her brain. Derek wasn't here. Maybe he'd gone to get breakfast for them.

Something seemed off as the silence dragged on, and

it finally hit her that Burnaby was gone, too. Hopefully, Derek had taken him for a walk. Another smile curved her lips. It appeared the puppy was making progress. Weakening him. And she hoped she was doing the same.

She sprang up from the makeshift bed with more optimism and energy than she'd had for ages. After searching all over for something to tie her tangled hair with, she remembered she had a clip in her purse, and put it to use. Then she went into the kitchen and started cleaning up the mess from her wasted cooking adventure.

The condo wasn't messy, really, beyond Derek's bedroom, but she could tell he hadn't spent much time taking care of it. A thick layer of dust covered every surface. Using a damp towel, she got rid of it.

She located an ancient vacuum cleaner in the hall closet and ran it over the floor of the carpeted rooms. As she worked, she found herself periodically checking out the sliding door to see if Derek and Burnaby were on their way in.

By the time she heard the door open, she'd scrubbed down the counters and tile floors, shined the mirrors and fixtures, and was working on the master bathroom.

Burnaby reached her first, at high speed, of course. She rubbed the sides of his face and baby-talked to him, letting him land a couple of licks on her cheek, which made her laugh.

Macey expected Derek to follow the dog in to find her, but he didn't appear. She headed to the kitchen. When she saw him, her heart fluttered.

He stood in the doorway, his back to her, looking out at the sparkling gulf. He'd taken his shirt off and held it in one hand, a can of pop in his other. He apparently hadn't heard her behind him. She couldn't help gaping at his body like a groupie, admiring his muscled arms, his wide shoulders, that powerful back. His skin shone with moisture and he was breathing fast, as if he'd been running.

From this view, it was easy to see the hero he was— the man who could handle any emergency situation. How could the man she saw have stopped believing in himself, maybe even stopped believing in life? Macey hoped with every fiber of her being that he was on the way to finding meaning in something. Any little thing.

"Hey," she said.

He started and faced her. "Figured you'd gone home."

She didn't know what she'd been expecting from him, but it was definitely a little more warmth. Not so much indifference.

"I'm leaving soon. I have to open at work. Just thought I'd tidy things for you."

Derek glanced around the open-concept dining area, kitchen and living room. Instead of a grateful smile, he frowned. "Why'd you do that?"

"Because it needed it."

"You didn't have to." He meant what he said. He wasn't giving her the obligatory polite objection.

"It was no big deal."

He walked around her and threw the now-empty can in the trash under the sink. He hadn't yet met her eyes.

"You better get out of here if you're going to make it on time."

She flinched. He really wanted her to leave. He couldn't care less whether she got to The Shell Shack on time or not; he just wanted her out of his condo.

Macey tried to hide the fact that she was stunned. Tried to cover her hesitation as she absorbed his between-the-lines message.

"Right. I'm leaving." She picked up her purse from the kitchen counter and nearly tripped over the dog.

Crap. The dog.

"What about Burnaby?" She reached down and ruffled the fur on his neck, more to comfort herself than him.

"He can stay."

She looked up sharply in surprise.

Derek wasn't happy about it, she could tell. That was fine as long as he gave the dog a good home.

Had she dreamed up last night and the intimacy they'd shared?

"There's a small bag of food here, but he'll go through it in about two days."

Derek nodded.

She pressed her lips together in frustration. "Did I do something wrong, Dare?" she asked, hating that her voice went high and squeaky.

He didn't answer her for so long she thought he was going to ignore her altogether. At last, when tears had filled her eyes and her throat had developed a lump the size of the Gulf of Mexico, he shook his head.

"Just have a lot to think about."

Something snapped inside of Macey. She was not going to stand by and let him retreat yet again, not after last night. She slammed her purse down on the table.

"Yeah. You do. Specifically, about how you treat the people around you. The very ones you've tried so hard to piss off so we'll leave you alone. When are you going to get it through your head that I'm not going to leave you alone, no matter how mean or indifferent you are to me?"

She could feel the heat in her face but wasn't about to back down.

"What do you want from me, Macey?"

"What do I *want?* Are you kidding?"

"You think since you stayed overnight I should let you move in? Is that why you cleaned the place?"

She took a slow, calming breath that actually didn't do a thing to settle her down. Her head throbbed in time with her pulse. "I don't want anything *from* you. I want something *for* you. Something like peace of mind. A flash of happiness now and then. That's all I want, Derek. Forgive me for cleaning. I was trying to be nice, but that seems to be a foreign concept to you."

"I didn't ask you to be nice. Matter of fact, I made it very clear I wasn't up for a visit when you came to town."

She picked up her purse again and hurried down the hall.

"Macey. Wait."

She ignored him, walking straight out the door. Tears burned her eyes again, but this time they were tears of anger. Regardless, though, she wasn't going to let him see her cry. Not this time. He'd seen her in tears countless instances over the years, but they had never been caused by him. This was different.

She walked along the edge of the street the whole way home, kicking the heck out of every rock she came across, imagining each one was Derek's head. His stinking, self-absorbed, hard head.

THERE HE WENT AGAIN, being the biggest goddamn bastard alive.

Waking up beside Macey had freaked him out—or rather, how much he'd liked it had freaked him out. He'd thought he'd gotten his wits back during the run along the beach, but when he came in here and saw how much she'd done to the place, he'd felt pinned down. Indebted. As if she expected something from him.

Neither one of them could afford to let her have expectations about anything concerning him. The sooner she understood that, the better. He just wished he'd found a way to get that point across without being his trademark asshole self.

He leaned down to Burnaby, who'd meandered over to his feet and dropped, pooped out from their exercise.

"I've rethought things, dog. Compared to a woman, you might make a damn fine roommate. I've got two steaks in the fridge. Let's have some lunch."

CHAPTER SEVENTEEN

HAVING THE ENTIRE DAY OFF was nothing but a hassle for Derek. What the hell was he supposed to do with all that time?

He'd gone to the grocery store, semi-inspired by the steaks he and the dog had devoured for lunch. Turned out he *was* sick of burgers and cocktail shrimp. He could cook just fine, thanks to a restaurateur mother and nights of feeding the guys at the fire station back in Dallas; he just hadn't bothered with it. Not once since he'd been on the island.

He'd decided to make spaghetti for dinner, with sauce from a jar. Wasn't as good as his mother's recipe, but it was still ten times better than more bar food. The Shell Shack's repertoire was okay, but day after day for several months…it did get old.

Now he and Burnaby had hours to kill before the never-ending day would be over. It seemed that Burnaby felt as penned up as Derek, being stuck inside the condo for the afternoon, so they took to the beach. They walked south with no particular destination in mind.

The beach was nearly deserted, likely because it was the dinner hour. Gulls circled overhead, their sporadic calls sounding like strategy sessions on where to find the best grub. The birds kept Burnaby entertained, making him ten kinds of crazy as he tried to figure out how to snatch one from the air. The fine sand was warm beneath Derek's bare feet although the sun was close to starting its descent.

The horizon was crisp in the distance tonight, and a large ship lurked at the edge of his vision. A little closer, a fishing boat crawled slowly along. The waves were relatively small, rolling in like a lullaby.

As they came upon The Shell Shack, Derek fought the urge to drop by and check on things. Macey was still there, about done with her shift, he knew. The only thing keeping him away was the chance of running into her.

He distanced himself from the bar by wading into knee-deep waves as they passed. Burnaby stretched his leash to the max to stay just out of reach of the rolling waves. Apparently he wasn't a water dog.

They wandered beyond Macey's apartment, farther south than Derek had ventured before. He was making all kinds of strides with beach exploration today, he realized. He'd just never thought to stroll along the sand before now, likely too wrapped up in himself and his grief. Straying so far from the condo was freeing and gave him a new perspective on a lot of things.

He was surprised when he saw the San Amaro Island Fire Station a good distance south of his bar. He hadn't realized the station was on the beach. Hadn't even considered checking it out before, but at the sight of it and the shiny red ladder truck standing at the ready, he felt an invisible force pulling him.

You miss it, don't you?

Had he wandered by the station before now, he likely would've turned back and avoided it. Now, though, he was curious.

Without conscious decision, he angled toward it.

The garage sat on the street side of the lot and opened on both the north and south ends, with the trucks parked parallel to the gulf. They had an engine and two trucks, one likely a backup, plus an ambulance and a water rescue unit. The living quarters of the station were on the beach side, with floor-to-ceiling windows lining a section he'd bet was the common area.

"Let's go pay the place a visit," he said to the dog, which didn't seem at all worried about where they were heading. Burnaby was too wrapped up in the gull drama, the blowing sea grasses and dog life in general.

Derek spotted the public door on the north side, surrounded by a courtyard with benches and a flagpole. As he got closer, he saw a firefighter in the garage loading something on the truck.

"Howdy," the guy called as Derek walked toward him, and he realized it was the man Macey had gone out with. Evan Drake. Didn't it figure that was the first person he'd run into.

Derek swallowed his annoyance and proceeded without hesitation. The guy had only taken her out once, as far as he knew. And Derek had just been with her all night.

"Evening," Derek said. "How's it going?"

"Not bad at all."

The guy was friendly enough. Always had been, for that matter. If he hadn't taken Macey on a date, he and Derek would probably get along like brothers. "You here to check things out? Thinking about joining us?"

"Just out for a walk. Haven't been this way before."

"Hey, boy." Evan leaned over and gave Burnaby a rubdown.

That he was well-acquainted with the dog drove home the point that as Macey's neighbor, he was part of her life, repeat dates or not. Derek's jaw tightened and he had to force himself to relax.

"Like to see the place?" Evan asked.

"Sure, if you've got time." He couldn't help himself. Now that he was here, he wanted to see everything, learn about how they operated.

Just out of curiosity. Nothing else.

Evan nodded and closed the compartment on the truck. "We're a fraction of the size of what you're used to, but we've got a pretty good setup here for what we need. Except for spring break—then we could use about four more stations."

"I can imagine the invasion of tourists."

"Thousands of idiot students who come down and drink for a week straight. Keeps us hopping for a whole month. Come on in."

"Got a place I could tie him up?" Derek asked, gesturing to Burnaby.

"You can bring him in. No one'll mind."

Derek called to the dog and followed Evan through the garage into the station itself. They went down a hallway, past several doorways, and came out in the living area. The windowed wall Derek had seen from the outside was indeed in the living room and afforded them a heck of a view.

Five men occupied the two couches and one of the easy chairs, most of them watching a baseball game on the large-screen television. One was reading a magazine.

"TV, library, video games," Evan said, gesturing.

"What's up, Evan?" the guy in the chair said.

"This is Derek…" He looked to Derek to supply his last name.

"Severson. I was with the Dallas Fire Department."

Derek recognized Macey's other friend, the guy who usually came to the bar with Evan.

"You remember Clay Marlow," Evan said, pointing to him. "That's Scott Pataki, Cole Tanner, Rafael Sandoval. Our captain, Joe Mendoza."

Each man stood, shook Derek's hand and acknowledged the knee-high black-and-white dog with a comment or a pat on the head. The canine lapped up the attention. Captain Mendoza came around the couch to Derek. "You on vacation?"

"Permanent resident," Derek said. "Run a bar up the beach a ways. The Shell Shack."

"I know the place," Captain Mendoza said, nodding. "Not fighting fires anymore?"

Derek shook his head. "Just helping out my uncle. He had to retire but can't seem to let go of the bar." Although it appeared he was starting to.

"We could use you here if you ever want to get back into it."

"I'll keep that in mind. Thank you." Derek kept his tone noncommittal but polite. Even though he wasn't prepared to jump back into firefighting, he appreciated the casual offer. Maybe in a few years he would take the captain up on it.

"I'll show you the rest," Evan said, leading him out of the living room.

Derek nodded to each man as they acknowledged him again with a good-night or a nice-to-meet-you.

"Kitchen's a little small—we've doubled in size in the past ten years as the island population has grown," Evan said, gesturing to the room that looked out on the court-yard. "We're overdue for an expansion but they haven't found space for it in the budget. We're doing well to get the equipment we need sometimes."

"Sounds familiar," Derek muttered. "They always want you to do a thousand-dollar job on a hundred-dollar budget."

"It's universal," Evan said, shaking his head.

The kitchen was neat but showed some wear and tear. The chairs around a long table in the center didn't all match. None of that mattered, though, Derek knew. Just the sight forced him to recall the camaraderie he'd been missing since leaving his own station. He'd bet anything the men here shared the same ties. That's what happened when you faced danger together. No matter how much you tried to explain to an outsider what you went through, no one would ever get it like another firefighter did.

Farther down the hall, in the fitness room, another two guys were working out, and Derek did a mental inventory of all their equipment. That was another thing he missed—having more than just his weight machine to stay in shape.

The next door led to a darkened conference and training room with a table, video screen and other electronics. Standard fare.

"Bunks are this way," Evan said, leading him back toward the kitchen and down a separate hallway. "Two beds per room. The john's at the end of the hall."

Derek spotted the two restroom doors. "You have any women in the department?" he asked.

"Not a one. Never have. I'm sure it won't be long, though."

"How many alarms does your department run?"

"Not nearly as many as Dallas. We have about eighty or ninety per month. Goes up seven hundred percent in March."

"Must be one hell of a month."

"Guys fight over taking vacations in April and May if that tells you anything."

They wandered outside through the garage, Burnaby alongside. Evan told Derek about a few of the stranger spring-break calls they'd had in the past few years, and they talked firefighting for a few more minutes.

"Suppose I better get the dog back home to settle down for the night," Derek said finally.

"Before you go," Evan said, his tone becoming more personal, "best of luck to you with Macey."

His words stopped Derek short. "We aren't together," he clarified, bending to adjust Burnaby's collar, even though it didn't need adjusting.

"She cares about you, man."

"Yeah. We've been friends since grade school. Grew up together." He tested the leash to make sure it was secure.

Evan nodded. "Goes beyond that, though."

"Nah. Just friends."

"Maybe, but she'd like more."

What was up with this guy? "You're the one she went out with."

He laughed. "Let's just say that was a dead end. Macey's great, don't get me wrong. But I'm not her kind of guy. I get the feeling she's looking for something a little more serious than I could give her."

Derek tended to agree. "She's not a casual dater. Never has been."

"That may be, but I think it's more a case of her having her eye on you."

Derek didn't stop to consider it. There was no point. "I'm not in any state to give her what she wants, either. That's one thing you and I have in common."

"I understand. Just wanted you to know I was stepping aside in case you're interested in her."

"Good to know." Derek shook the other man's hand. "Thanks for the tour."

"See you around."

Derek and Burnaby strolled back out to the beach toward home.

Interested in Macey. Not the words he would've chosen. Cared a great deal about her, yes. Turned on by her, hell yeah. Considering his long-term potential or lack thereof, though, any interest he had was pointless.

CHAPTER EIGHTEEN

IF MACEY COULD GET through today, she could do just about anything.

She'd stayed up nearly till dawn working on a grant proposal for her nonprofit. It wasn't that the proposal had to be done anytime soon. It was more that she'd desperately needed a distraction from her thoughts, all of which involved Derek. No shock there.

She'd actually tried to go to bed early after a long, busy shift at the bar, but Derek hadn't let her. Not in a technical sense; she hadn't heard a single word from him after she'd left his condo yesterday morning. Naively, she'd thought for sure he would come into work during her shift to apologize for the way he'd blown her off.

Stretched out in bed, she'd alternated between heated anger at the way he'd dismissed her yesterday morning, and memories of lying in his arms the night before, which induced heat of an entirely different kind. A half hour of tossing, turning and trying to shut out all thoughts of him had been her limit. She'd dragged her laptop to bed and set to work.

She was driving to the bar today because she'd slept in and ended up rushing around to get ready on time. Her shift was noon to nine, and she knew Derek would be there for most of it, as he'd opened this morning. Strangely, his truck wasn't in its usual spot outside the bar. Macey pulled up and took his place, wondering if he was MIA again. While she didn't want anything bad to happen to him, a reprieve from working side by side for several hours would be welcome.

Welcome but not going to happen.

Burnaby was lying in the shade of the building just outside the door. Macey bent to rub his belly. She spotted Derek wiping down the bar before she even set foot inside the homey shack with the faint beer aroma. Her clueless heart sped up, seemingly only capable of recalling how they'd spent the night together and not how he'd acted afterward. Her mind was much more ready to face the facts, though.

She braced herself to be as indifferent as possible toward him and yet friendly enough that he wouldn't figure out how much he'd hurt her.

As if they were just coworkers.

"Afternoon," she said as he joined her behind the bar.

"Hey." He didn't look at her and she bit her tongue to keep from saying more.

Andie was at the grill, cooking up three or four orders, and after clocking in, Macey stepped up to the counter to wait on people in the line that had suddenly formed at the register.

Two hours and about two hundred customers later, Derek and Macey had exchanged a grand total of approximately four sentences. All work related. And that was fine with her—or at least she tried to tell herself it was.

Andie wandered out of the back room to refill her drink. Derek was straightening the liquor bottles on the shelves while Macey wiped down the main counter and joked with some of the customers sitting at the bar.

"Derek," Andie said. "We're out of tomatoes and almost out of lettuce. You need to run to the store."

He shot her a look. "If I'm the boss, shouldn't I be giving out the orders instead of taking them from you?"

Andie shrugged. "If that makes you feel better. But we need veggies. Stat."

Normally Macey would've volunteered to run the errand, but it turned out she didn't feel like being helpful today. She focused on scrubbing some dried ketchup off the counter. She could sense Derek staring at her back, but she didn't give in.

"Guess I'll go get the veggies," he said finally.

Macey ignored him and he left without another word.

"Thank God he's gone," Andie said. "What is with the two of you?"

"What do you mean?" Macey asked, throwing the towel in a tub of hot soapy water on the floor.

"Something happened between you guys again. You're making me crazy."

Macey had tried to act unaffected by Derek, if a little less talkative than usual. She gladly stepped up to the counter as a sunburned man ordered a drink. Andie leaned on the doorjamb watching her, waiting until she'd drawn the guy's beer and taken his money.

"You going to tell me?"

Macey turned and met Andie's gaze. "You're not usually one to butt in and demand details about other people's lives. What's going on?"

"Are you kidding? I've watched for several weeks while you two dance around your feelings and act like there's a sane reason you haven't jumped into bed together. I want you to get it over with already. Put the rest of us out of our misery."

Macey glanced around. Fortunately, everyone seemed to be involved in their own conversations.

"If I told you we slept together, would you leave it alone?"

"What?" Andie's eyes widened and then she smiled smugly. "I knew it. Congrats."

"We *slept* together. As in slumbered. Side by side. Nothing else happened."

"You shared a bed and nothing happened? Is he dead?"

"Unfortunately, I think so."

"What happened?"

Macey assured herself there was no one waiting for a drink or a burger, then moved closer and told Andie the gist of her night at Derek's condo.

"So now he's barely talking to you." Andie frowned.

"He's acting like *I* should apologize. I'm trying to pretend I'm not ready to strangle him. He wants to make me mad. Wants me to leave him alone. But I won't do that."

Andie took a sip and beckoned Macey back into the kitchen. She scooped chips and cheese sauce into a cardboard container and put it on the counter between them. "You're getting to him."

"I'm lucky he hasn't fired me yet."

"You need to seduce him."

Macey nearly choked on the chip she'd just shoved into her mouth. "About like I need to go lie down in the middle of interstate traffic in Dallas."

"Maybe if you got it over with, things could go back to normal between you two."

"You forget that Derek's not his normal self. With good reason. There *is* no normal between us anymore." Macey had to struggle not to think too hard about Andie's suggestion, not to give it any life at all in her mind, because if she did, it would taunt her all night.

Andie dug a jalapeño pepper out of the refrigerated tub and stacked it on her cheese-drenched chip. "So what are you going to do?"

Macey swirled a chip in the cheese, pondering the question she'd been asking herself since she'd gotten here. "I'm going to jump him."

Seeing Andie's pretty brown eyes bulge out of her head was worth the fib.

"Or more likely option B—just let him be for a couple days and then get back to being nice and forgiving," Macey said. "I'm leaving in a little over a week. I can't take off with him still just as messed up as he was when I got here."

"He's not."

"You don't think so?"

"Before you got here, I'd never seen him laugh. Not sure he'd even smiled. And now you've got him taking care of a dog."

Macey grinned, feeling as if Burnaby *had* been a victory. Maybe the only one, but she'd take it.

"You've definitely been good for him, Macey."

Right now, she felt she'd been anything *but* good for Derek. And time was a-ticking.

DEREK WAS COUNTING THE days until Macey went back to Dallas.

As soon as she left, he could stop becoming sidetracked by the sight of her and those curves she'd always kept hidden in the past. He could stop trying to catch the scent of her hair, quit recalling how she'd felt in his arms. Most importantly, he could stop feeling guilty for pushing her away.

Once she left, things could get back to normal around here…whatever normal was. He could admit he'd miss having her at the bar. They'd slipped back into making the hours pass faster when they worked together, just like in high school at their mothers' restaurant. At least up until the last few days and his resolution to put distance between them.

As if he'd conjured her, he spotted her walking up the bar's concrete stairs from the beach. His eyes locked on her against his will. She couldn't see him yet so he watched her.

He nearly swallowed his tongue as she came closer. She wore a bikini with a wrap around her hips, showing off her flat, sexy middle and allowing him the best view he'd ever had of her breasts, excluding when they'd been bare in her bedroom. The modest orange-and-yellow top left very little to his imagination, but his imagination was on overtime, anyway. His first thought was why in the hell had she been hiding all these years? His body responded without his permission, and he was glad for the counter standing between him and the rest of the world.

On the heels of his initial *wow* was the conviction that she was showing too much to the rest of the world. Several men noticed her and Derek had the primal urge to battle each one of them.

He didn't have the right to compliment her *or* protect her. Best-case scenario for her would be someone else protecting her from *him*.

MACEY DIDN'T SEE MUCH of anything as she climbed the steps to The Shell Shack. She was deeply involved in a mind game where she pretended she was full of courage, and that asking Derek to do anything wasn't putting herself in a vulnerable, scary position. It was hard to hide from the truth—that she cared too much.

She'd let three days pass since she'd told Andie she was going to back off before the last big hurrah.

Today was the hurrah.

As she moved the short distance from the doorway to the bar, she became aware of people watching her. Two or three men followed her with their eyes, and she felt exposed in her swimsuit and sarong. She should've kept her tank on but she'd flown out of her apartment in a hurry and, okay, maybe had hoped showing some skin would affect Derek. He couldn't be totally numb to her—not the way he'd reacted when they'd kissed. At the time she'd had no doubt he was just as into it as she was, but now, days later, she was unsure. Insecure. But who could fault her after his latest rejection?

When she zeroed in on Derek, his eyes were glued to her, making her breath hitch. As she neared the counter, a customer standing at the bar a few feet away hollered to get Derek's attention.

He nodded at Macey once to let her know he'd be back to her, and took the customer's order. Charlotte waved from behind the bar but didn't stop to chat.

Macey's insecurity gnawed at her. How did she so easily slip back into her pre-Peace Corps self when she was around Derek? Time to buck up and be a big girl. She was absolutely confident she was doing the right thing in inviting him out.

"Hey," he said as soon as he finished with the customer.

"Hi." She forced a smile and did her best to make it look natural and free. "Busy day?"

"Swamped until thirty minutes ago. Hot. People are thirsty."

"You're working a short shift, right?"

"Yes, ma'am. You should know. You wrote the schedule."

She caught his eyes lowering to her chest and felt encouraged. "I was wondering if you'd do me a favor...."

She saw his body tense, but wasn't about to give up now. "I'm leaving in a few days so I figured it's time to do some of the things I've been wanting to."

"What is it, Mace?"

"I have a lesson in the art of sand castle building at four. Will you go with me?"

"I work until four."

"I know. I'm meeting the teacher up the beach, close to your condo. You could join us as soon as you get out of here." She silently willed him to say yes. "Please? Last crazy tourist thing I'll ask you to do with me. Promise."

She noticed she was holding her breath, so released it slowly as she leaned her elbows on the bar. Derek's eyes flashed down to her cleavage again, only for a second, but it sent a current of heat straight to her core.

She was an idiot. This was going to hurt so much when she finally went back to Dallas, to the new life she'd anticipated for months. Suddenly it didn't seem like everything she'd been looking forward to. But she'd known from the beginning that this could be difficult, she reminded herself. She still wouldn't do anything differently if given the chance. Maybe Andie was right and she'd done Derek a little bit of good in some way. If so, it was worth the potential—make that inevitable—heartache.

"It'll be fun. The guy is really good, Dare. What's not to like about building a sand castle?"

"Never been the sand castle type, I guess. It'll just wash away with the tide."

"We'll take pictures. You're not going to make me do this all by my lonesome, are you?"

He glanced around and spotted a woman approaching the far side of the bar to place an order. Charlotte stepped in to help her.

"Fine," he said. "We'll build sand castles. I'll meet you there."

She smiled, this time unforced. His agreement made her want to throw her fist in the air and say "yes!" She refrained, though, and tried to play it as no big deal. He didn't have to know she planned to extend it into a casual dinner together and maybe even a movie rental afterward.

He shook his head, the corners of his lips turning up despite his grumpy mood, she'd bet. She felt too giddy for the circumstances. But she'd won. She had a non-date with Derek. One last chance to try to make things comfortable between them and hopefully to make him laugh, remind him how to have fun.

CHAPTER NINETEEN

DEREK WAS BEYOND dead meat.

Macey's hour-long sand castle lesson had just ended and he'd missed every last minute of it. She'd missed a good chunk of it, too, because she'd been so preoccupied. The Sand Man, her teacher—who refused to tell her any other name—had finally asked if everything was okay. She'd lied that it was, but he knew she'd been stood up. If she wasn't so angry she'd be humiliated.

The Sand Man had left her several tools of the trade—a brush, straw, spatula, mini shovel and chisel—as part of what she'd paid for. Her creation, a compact but detailed fortress with four towers, was almost finished. She refused to walk off and leave it without finalizing the crenellations at the top of the walls and the moat. If she had any real talent for sculpting, she would add knights and dragons to shoot anyone who came too close. Just the kind of mood she was in.

As she bent over the exterior staircase to chisel the edges, a long shadow suddenly stretched over her, blocking out the sun. She knew without looking that Derek had finally seen fit to show up. She continued working, determined to ignore him for as long as it took to get rid of him.

Forever and a half seemed to tick by and neither of them spoke. Macey didn't even glance up to make sure it was him.

She finished the stair details and was so sidetracked by his presence she didn't know what to do next.

The moat. She went to work squaring the sides, carving out slices of sand with one of the tools the Sand Man had taught her to use.

Derek moved at last, startling her. He sat down close to the castle, on the opposite side from where Macey was working. This put him less than three feet away from her and still she pretended to be alone, having the time of her ever-loving life carving sand out of the moat.

"Macey." She involuntarily made eye contact, but turned away quickly, scolding herself for the automatic reaction.

"I'm sorry."

As ticked off as she was, a truckful of Hostess Cupcakes wouldn't help his cause.

"Macey!" Louder now. He was getting mad.

Pity.

"I got caught up at the bar. The TV guy showed up to install the two televisions and I wanted to make sure everything went okay. Then I had to take the dog home."

"Andie could've babysat the TV guy."

He beat his first two fingers on his thigh. "I suppose she could have. I wanted to make sure he did it the way I wanted him to."

Macey took her time cleaning out freshly fallen sand

from the bottom of the moat. "So your TVs are more important than me."

"Of course not."

Her fury built like the power in a wave, deceivingly calm on the outside but ready to twist someone's neck beneath the surface.

"It's just a sand castle, Mace. We can build one anytime."

She jumped to her feet, tossed her tools into her beach bag and stomped off toward her apartment.

"Macey."

She kept going, digging her feet into the sand with each step, clenching her teeth until her head throbbed.

"Dammit, Macey, wait up!"

She heard him jogging up behind her, and picked up her own pace. Seconds later, he caught her by the wrist and pulled her to a stop. Macey swung her arm away from him with all her strength. "Don't touch me."

"Calm down. What's really going on here? This can't be about learning to build a sand castle."

She stared at him, breathing hard, trembling.

"This," she said quietly, "is about you letting me down. You treating me like crap for the past week. You telling me you were going to do something and then flaking. Standing me up. Embarrassing me, and worse, letting me know just how important our friendship isn't."

"I…"

"I've tried, Derek. Tried to be nice, and when that didn't go over so well, I just tried to be sympathetic and remember what you're going through. But you know what? I don't care what kind of grief and pain you have, nothing justifies letting your friends down." She realized she was poking his chest as she spoke.

"I never asked for anything from you, Macey."

"You never asked for it but you needed it. You need something, Derek, although it's obviously something I can't give you." She was just short of yelling. People were starting to stare, but she didn't care.

"I knew this wouldn't be easy. But I thought our friendship could handle just about anything. I guess I was wrong, because I can't try anymore. There. Have it your way. I'm done."

Again, he caught her by the wrist, both of them, actually, and moved closer. "Macey, stop for a second. Take a breath—"

"I don't want a breath!" She tried to whip her arms away, but this time he was prepared. Tears formed in her eyes but she couldn't even wipe them away because he held her hands, and was much stronger than her.

"I'm sorry. I screwed up. Over and over." He hesitated, swallowing hard while his eyes searched hers. "You're the one person in this world I never wanted to screw up with, and now I've hurt you. I..." He swore to himself. "I'm sorry, Macey. So damn sorry."

Her shoulders sagged and she suddenly felt so darn tired, as if she could sleep for a week. But she wasn't ready to make peace with him. Didn't have the energy. She closed her eyes until he let go of her, then she dropped to the sand, cradling her knees to her chest.

Derek sat next to her, his thigh right near hers but not quite touching. She noticed that detail but wasn't sure how she felt about it. Didn't know if she wanted him to touch her.

She stared out at the cresting waves, mesmerized by their rhythm. Calmed by their repetitiveness.

"I was trying to protect you," Derek said after several minutes had passed.

Macey closed her eyes. She'd always loved Derek's protective streak, but how treating her like garbage equated protection, she could hardly wait to hear. "What, pray tell, were you protecting me from?"

Derek chuckled humorlessly. "Some asshole who's walking around in a fog, so wrapped up in his own problems that he doesn't worry about anyone else."

Macey nodded. "I've met the type before. Scumbags, every last one of them."

"Complete bastards," he agreed.

"They deserve to be burned at the stake."

Derek cringed beside her. "Maybe we could go for a single bullet wound instead?"

"Too easy."

He hesitated. "I don't trust myself right now. I'm impossible to be around, and that's why I've tried to distance myself."

"I came down here knowing you'd be hard to be around, Dare."

"I never said anything I've done was the right thing. Just trying to tell you where I'm coming from."

"I never expected anything from you except common decency."

"And I blew that."

"Pretty much."

"I'm working on it, Macey. I want to feel better. This grief sucks."

That he was tired of hurting was a step. Before now, she'd gotten the impression he wanted to suffer.

"What you said about the building collapsing the other night," he continued, "it helped."

"Really?" She couldn't hide her shock that anything she'd done had helped…and that he'd admit it.

"You're right about there being some things we can't prevent or control. It's something we learn in the academy. Sometimes all we can ever do is react to situations to the best our training has prepared us for. There'll be times when we do everything by the book and we still don't win the battle."

"This was one of those times," Macey said quietly.

He nodded slowly, staring into the distance. "I think it was." After a couple of minutes, he got to his feet. "Enough of this sad crap. Your castle needs finishing touches."

Macey stood, too. "Yeah, but what do you know about sand castle building?"

"Hate to tell you this, Mace, but it doesn't require a big fancy class with the sand god."

"Sand Man."

"What?"

"The Sand Man gave me my lesson."

Derek grinned, then chuckled and shook his head. "Come on, I'll show you sand man."

He held his hand out and she took it with only a momentary hesitation.

"So am I forgiven?" Derek asked as they approached the castle. "Or do I still need to grovel some more?"

"Oh, you'll need to grovel quite a bit more. Maybe feed me later."

"I know this great little place on the beach that serves burgers and cocktail shrimp…."

"Sorry. Too easy."

"You drive a hard bargain, woman."

"You have a lot to make up for."

Derek released her hand and circled the castle, eyeing it critically. "This tower needs a remodel."

"The tower's fine."

He shook his head. "And the moat looks good about halfway around. Then it gets sloppy."

"The construction foreman was rudely interrupted by an inconsiderate jerk when she was working on it."

"You start on the moat, sand chick, and I'll make this tower into a…tower."

ROUGHLY AN HOUR LATER, they declared the castle to be finished. Derek combed the litter near a trash can on the beach, found a scrap from a paper bag and made a flag with the straw from the Sand Man. He inserted it into the tallest tower and declared it "Castle Locke."

"Someday I want a life-size version of it," Macey said.

"Didn't figure you to be the princess type."

"Every girl wants to be a princess deep down."

"I'll keep that in mind," Derek said, unable to ignore how unprincesslike she looked. Princesses brought to mind little-girl charm and pink ribbons. Macey, in that bikini, had shed all her little-girl anything.

He tore his attention away from her curves and smoothed out the point where the flag stuck into the top of the tower. Grains of sand tumbled down the side from his touch—just a few.

And then some more.

And then the whole damn tower split in half and crashed to a lump of nothing.

"My fortress!" Macey covered her mouth with her hand, her eyes wide.

Derek tried to hold back a grin, not because the castle had collapsed but because of her obvious horror.

"Macey, it's okay. Just a sand castle."

"I paid a hundred and fifty bucks for that castle. Plus labor."

One hundred fifty bucks? For a sand castle lesson? The girl was a head case. A very sexy one, but a head case at any rate. He couldn't help laughing.

She punched his arm. "Castle wrecker!"

"The only thing to do is destroy it all the way."

"What?"

"Try it. Might feel good. Take a running jump right into it."

"I could fix it," she said stubbornly, circling to the other side to survey the damage.

He bent to look closely at the collapsed tower as Macey reached his other side. "It'd take hours to fix it."

"I've got time," she declared.

Derek glanced up at her, shook his head, then faced the castle again. Just as he reached out to salvage the flag, he felt himself tipping forward, courtesy of Macey's foot connecting with his ass. He had no choice but to land right on top of her masterpiece. Ex-masterpiece.

Behind him, Macey laughed. He rolled to his back, ruining the castle completely, and stared up at her, shielding his eyes from the low sun behind her.

"You were absolutely right," she said, snickering. "That did feel good."

He stared wordlessly at her for several moments, then sprang to his feet. No way was she *not* going to pay for that. Macey reacted quickly and darted toward the water. He rushed in behind her, even though he wasn't wearing swim trunks. Probably destroyed his tennis shoes, but what the hell. Sweet revenge.

Macey hollered, a cross between a screech and a laugh, as he almost caught up with her. Then she torpedoed into a wave and escaped. His shoes were dragging him down, being sucked into the sand with each step.

She surfaced, and when she stood, the water was just above her waist, giving him an excellent view of the way her wet bikini top clung, outlining her nipples.

"You're going to pay eventually, Mace." He forced his eyes from her chest, which seemed to be something he had to do a lot. "Whether it's now or later, you're going down."

"Trembling in fear here." She laughed and dived away again.

Derek would've followed her but his shoes were a serious handicap. He trudged back to dry land and removed them, his socks and his drenched T-shirt. He picked up the beach bag Macey had jumped over during her escape, and found her large beach towel inside. He pulled it out and wiped his face dry, looking at Macey, who'd swum farther out. He lowered himself to the sand, catching his breath and preferring to watch her rather than chase her. For the time being.

Still in waist-deep water, she was trying to jump over waves. Her smile was visible from here and he realized a grin was finding its way across his face, as well. How could it not, as he saw how into the moment she was, how much fun she could have just playing in the waves like a kid. Sometimes he wondered what it would be like to be so carefree, but he'd never been close to it, even before Julie's death.

Derek hadn't felt this relaxed in ages. Clearing the air with Macey had done wonders for his mood. He hadn't realized how heavily the additional guilt of trying to push her away had weighed on him. He didn't deserve for her to be so forgiving, but he was damn glad.

He had only a few more days till she left.

Macey kept getting farther out. It looked as if she

could no longer touch the bottom. Her head bobbed in the water, but that was all.

Derek straightened as she went under again. She was getting too far out. He stood up to see her better, alarm prickling his neck. Her head went below the surface again, and he took several steps forward as he waited for her to come up.

CHAPTER TWENTY

DAMMIT, SHE WAS DOWN too long. Derek waded into the water, eyes glued to where he'd last seen her. Finally, Macey's head came up, but not long enough for her to get a good breath. Something was wrong.

Riptides. He'd heard customers at the bar talk about currents that sneaked up on people and carried them away from shore. The way to handle them, he'd heard, was not to try to swim against them. You had to move parallel to the shore and you'd eventually get out of the current.

It appeared Macey didn't know this or hadn't figured out what was happening.

Derek ran until he got to water deep enough to dive into. He hadn't swum for years, but sliced through the water as fast as he could, thanks in part to some serious adrenaline. It seemed a mile out to where Macey was. He was not going to let anything happen to her. Had to get there. Had to keep going.

He treaded water for a couple of seconds to spot her again, then swam full out. He thanked God he'd kept working out, even though he didn't use his body on the job anymore. The force of the current helped carry him to her even faster.

At last he reached her and saw her go under yet again. He put his arms around her torso and held her up so she could get a breath. She was still moving but he could tell she was wiped out. He pulled her across his body, her head cradled on his shoulder so she could get all the air she needed.

"It's okay, Macey. You're safe. I've got you."

She went limp in his arms and he checked to make sure she was still conscious. Her eyes fluttered open and she focused on him briefly before closing them again. Thank God. She'd make it. Now he just needed to get her to shore.

He slowly carried her south, not sure how to tell when they were out of the dangerous current. Finally he made it to where he could touch bottom. As soon as he got to water waist-deep, he picked Macey up and cradled her. She held on to his neck, which was a good sign.

He carried her to the dry sand and looked around, trying to get his bearings. They'd gone farther south than he'd thought. He could see the fire station a quarter of a mile down the beach. If they were closer, the guys at the station could help, but Derek wasn't about to leave her and go that far.

Gently, he put Macey on the sand. She was starting to shiver uncontrollably. He needed to get her into dry clothes and warm her up. Her bag was likely a half mile or more away and wasn't going to do them any good, either.

There were very few people on this section of beach right now, as it was dinnertime.

"I'm cold, Dare," Macey groaned, rolling to her side and curling up in a ball. "Tired."

"I'm going to get you a towel. Stay right here."

He jogged over to the closest group of people, a family with four rambunctious kids playing football. A woman sat under a large blue-and-white beach umbrella and alternated between watching the game and reading a paperback. Once he told her what had happened, she gave him one of the kids' towels. SpongeBob SquarePants to the rescue. He thanked her and asked where she and her family were staying. He intended to give them a new towel at the very least. Later. When Macey was taken care of.

He hurried back to wrap the towel around her.

"Th-thank y-you. Who t-turned off the s-sun?"

Derek smiled and picked her up, towel and all. "Let's get you home. A warm bath and some sleep is what you need."

She rested her head on his shoulder as Derek made his way off the sand to the street. She wasn't heavy but he was glad her apartment was only a block and a half away.

As he walked through the small parking lot toward the stairs to her place, he spotted Evan on the second floor walkway, leaning over the railing and drinking a beer.

"Everything all right?" Evan called out.

Derek nodded. He climbed the stairs with Macey still in his arms and only paused for a moment to say, "She got caught up in a riptide. She's okay."

Evan rushed toward them. "You sure? She looks pale."

"She is. Never lost consciousness, though, thank God."

"Anything I can do?"

Derek shook his head. "Thanks." He kept going toward her door, then stopped and swore. "Her bag is on the beach. I'm sure her key is in the bag."

Macey blinked her eyes open. "It is."

"I've got a key," Evan said, and Derek told himself this was not the time to wonder what the hell Evan was doing with a key to her apartment.

"They let Burn out when I was working," Macey said quietly.

Okay then. He was a petty jealous bastard to worry about that when Macey was in bad shape. He was just glad they could get into her apartment so she could recover.

Evan came out of his place and unlocked Macey's door. "You want some dry clothes for yourself?"

Derek realized his shorts were soaked and his shoes and shirt were still on the beach. "Shorts would be great. Thanks, man."

Derek took Macey into her bedroom and lowered her to the bed.

A couple of minutes later, Evan poked his head in. "Key's on the kitchen counter. I'm going after her bag. What's it look like?"

"Rainbow tie-dye," Derek recalled.

"It says San Amaro Island on it," Macey added. "There's a bunch of sand castle tools inside."

"Got it. If you need anything else, we're the last unit on this level. Don't hesitate."

Derek nodded in appreciation. "She just needs to rest."

"Take care, Macey."

She mumbled something unintelligible.

"I'll see myself out," Evan said.

Once he was gone, Derek sat on the edge of the bed. "How you doing?"

"Okay." She opened her eyes. "Thanks for saving me, Dare."

His throat swelled up as he imagined what could have happened if he hadn't realized she was in trouble. He couldn't get any words out, so he trailed his knuckle down her cheek.

"Still a hero," Macey whispered.

He shook his head. "I did what anyone would've done."

"Dare?"

"Yeah?"

"Shut up."

He brushed her wet hair back from her face. "Ready to warm up with a bath?"

When she nodded, Derek took the shorts Evan had left and went in to start the water for her. He found bubble bath on the edge of the tub and added some to the running water. The lilac scent of it was so like Macey he actually sat there breathing it in for a couple of seconds.

Then he searched around and found an oversize, fluffy bath towel in the cabinet under the sink and set it on the floor next to the tub. Stripping, he hung his damp shorts up to dry, then pulled on the borrowed cutoff sweats. When the tub was full, he turned off the spigot and went back into the bedroom.

"Water's ready for you."

Macey sat up slowly, dazed and dopey.

"You okay?" he asked. "Do you need help?" He'd do whatever she needed him to, but if that included peeling her swimsuit off her and getting her into the tub he was going to have one hell of an uncomfortable evening.

"I can do it. I'm okay, Dare. Just tired."

She stood and reached behind her to untie her top. Derek turned away in a panic. Now was not the time for an eyeful.

"I'll be in the kitchen trying to find some dinner."

"Good luck," she said behind him. "Refrigerator's empty."

The urge to turn around and look at her was overwhelming; he was absolutely sure she was at least half-naked now. God help him. He forced his feet to move him out of the room.

Macey wasn't exaggerating when she said there wasn't much in the fridge. A tub of butter and two orange sodas—that was all. The freezer was bare. She was as bad as he was about feeding herself at home.

Chinese it was, then. He dug up a phone book in one of the kitchen drawers and called a place that advertised delivery. He didn't know exactly what Macey liked so he ordered four different dinners, plus egg rolls, crab rangoon and wonton soup. After he hung up, he sat there on the couch thinking about the day. They'd been through the wringer. He could feel his exhaustion in every last muscle. Maybe tonight he would sleep soundly once again.

The silence of the apartment suddenly registered and he realized he hadn't heard anything from Macey. No water splashing, no tub draining…nothing. He hopped up and rushed to the bathroom door.

"Mace?" He knocked softly with one knuckle.

She didn't respond.

"Macey. You okay?"

Still no answer. He barged through the door. Her head was above the surface, barely, and her eyes blinked open. She sat up, confused.

"What are you doing?" she asked, becoming more alert.

"You…what are *you* doing?" As soon as he knew she was okay, he couldn't help noticing her breasts, half-covered in suds. His body reacted immediately.

She looked around her. "I think I fell asleep."

"I thought you drowned," he said. He knelt by the tub and took her hand. "Don't do that to me, Mace. One scare in a day is plenty."

She relaxed against the back of the tub again, not seeming to mind being exposed. Derek didn't mind, either, unless you considered the blood rushing south with no relief in sight.

"Will you help me wash my hair?" Macey asked. "I'm

too tired to stand up and run the shower, but I need to get the salt water out of it."

Derek spotted a bottle of shampoo on a shelf above her head. He stood to get it, knowing if she opened her eyes and looked in the right place, she would see exactly how turned on he was. Her eyes were closed, though.

He took the drinking cup next to the sink and used it to pour water over her head. He put a dab of shampoo into his palm and lathered it up, then began massaging it into Macey's hair. She bent toward him, leaning on the side of the tub and resting her cheek on her arm so he could reach her better. The whole time she kept her eyes closed, and he could tell by the look on her face she was content. More than content.

He took his time working the soap through every part of her long hair, rubbing her scalp, her temples, her neck. After he rinsed out the shampoo, she pointed to the other bottle on the shelf and muttered something about conditioner.

He retrieved that bottle and started the process all over again. He combed his fingers through the sleek, slippery strands of her hair, loving the feel of it. He supported her neck in his hand as he poured water over her to rinse the conditioner out.

"Your water's getting cool. Why didn't you tell me?"

She sat up straight and glanced around her as if coming out of a trance. "I didn't notice. That felt so good. Thank you."

He reached between her feet to drain the tub and

realized she'd been in so long that the bubbles had mostly disappeared, which made her entire body visible. He closed his eyes briefly and begged God for strength.

She started to stand and he held his hand out to help her up. Then he bent down to get the big towel and to spread out the bath mat. As she climbed out of the tub, he steadied her with his hands on her narrow waist.

"I'm fine, Dare. But you're welcome to help me." The smile she gave him hinted at mischief. Did she know what she was doing to him? Was she enjoying this torture?

Because he was. Too much.

He held out the towel and wrapped it around her when she turned her back to him. He risked pressing a quick kiss to the side of her neck before stepping away. He was not going to make a move on her after she'd nearly drowned.

At that moment, a knock sounded on the door in the living room.

"Dinner," he said, having forgotten about that hunger. "Get some clothes on and join me."

MACEY'S BODY STILL tingled from having Derek help her bathe. The scalp massage had been sensuous and erotic. The way he'd caressed her with a slow, gentle touch… she'd imagined him touching other parts of her body with such tenderness.

She no longer cared how stupid it would be to sleep with Derek. She wouldn't have another chance once she left the island. It was now or never, and even though she knew it would be a one-time thing if it happened, she much preferred the pain of having him and then saying goodbye to him over passing up the chance to be with him. Besides, maybe some good sex would help him temporarily forget his woes. She didn't aim to take Julie's place by any means. Just to distract him.

As much as she wanted Derek, she was having trouble making the first move. She'd never been sexually aggressive and was too shy to take bold action. It'd been hard enough asking him to wash her hair, even though there was technically nothing sexual about it.

If the way her body throbbed was "nothing sexual," then she was in for trouble if Derek actually did pick up on her signals and give her what she needed.

Macey finished drying her body and toweled her hair as well as she could, then went to the closet in her room and pulled out her pink terry-cloth robe. There was nothing sexy about it, but she didn't really own anything sexy. And she wasn't ready to be that obvious. She wanted Derek to feel what she was feeling without any props or contrived setups.

She ran a pick through her damp hair as quickly as she could, feeling exhausted and weak from her unfortunate disagreement with the gulf.

"There you are," he said when she entered the kitchen. "I was beginning to wonder if you'd passed out again."

There were enough cardboard boxes of Chinese food to feed the entire apartment complex and then some.

"Hope you're hungry," he said as he took out two dinner plates from the cabinet next to the sink.

"A little. Actually, a lot, now that I smell it."

She heaped both fried and steamed rice on her plate, plus garlic chicken and pepper beef. An egg roll and two crab rangoons. She left all the soup for him.

"Hungry much?" Derek said from behind, looking over her shoulder. She could feel his breath on her neck and she shivered.

"Suddenly famished. Thanks for stocking up."

"I thought there was enough for two or more meals, but that was before you tore into it."

They ate on the living room floor, leaning against the couch. Derek quizzed her—skeptically, she could tell—about her sand castle lesson and the tips the Sand Man had passed along.

Macey didn't end up eating all the food she'd taken. Halfway through the meal, she set her plate on the end table and stretched out on the couch, fatigue settling into every inch of her.

The next thing she knew, she was in her bed with Derek not even a foot away from her.

CHAPTER TWENTY-ONE

DEREK WAS SLEEPING lightly enough that he felt Macey turn over to face him. He smelled her shampoo and lilac scent as she moved closer.

He was a glutton for punishment.... Otherwise why would he be in the same bed as her?

He'd carried her here with every intention of returning to the living room and sleeping on the couch. She was okay now, her brush with danger was over and everything was fine, but he hadn't wanted to leave her. When she'd tugged at him sleepily as he tucked her in, he'd been so easily swayed he should be ashamed. He'd quickly put the food away and cleaned their dishes, got her bag and his clothes from Evan, then climbed in next to her.

Macey ran her fingers over his bare arm now and he realized she wasn't just shifting in her sleep. She was more awake than he'd thought. A light outside cast just enough of a glow that he could make out her face, a mere two inches from his.

"Dare..."

"You're supposed to be sleeping." It was one of the dumbest things he'd ever said to a woman in bed with him.

"I slept. Hard." She trailed her fingers to his chest. "I didn't want you to leave tonight."

"Shh. I'm here."

Stupid move number two: he reached out and pulled her even closer. He could feel her warm body, still in the fuzzy robe, along the length of his. Then he felt a bare leg curling over his. His body sprang to life and there was no hiding how he felt.

Before he could give himself yet another round of the you-aren't-going-to-take-advantage-of-her-after-she-nearly-drowned talk, Macey's lips were on his, decisive and insistent. There was half a second when he considered stopping her, but then he gave himself over to the hunger he'd tried to deny for weeks.

Their tongues tangled, explored, slid over teeth, lips, each other. He felt a primal urge to taste every last inch of her. He trailed his lips over her jawline to her ear and nibbled on it, making Macey suck in her breath and then let out her pleasure in the most alluring sound—half sigh and half moan—he'd ever heard.

He couldn't keep his hands off her, every bit of her. She untied her robe and opened it, and he slid the sleeves off her arms one at a time. When he'd freed her from it, he tossed it to the floor and pulled her on top of him. Her breasts spilled over his chest and he palmed them as she returned her lips to his. He found one nipple and teased it, beaded it between his finger and thumb, feeling it pebble under his touch. He drew her upward so he could replace his fingers with his tongue.

In all the years he'd known Macey, he'd never once

guessed she'd be this responsive and passionate in bed. She wasn't shy with him in the least, contrary to what he would've expected. As if she needed to drive that point home, she slid his shorts over his aching shaft and down his legs, threw them over her shoulder, then took him in her mouth.

Sweet heaven. She was going to kill him and he was going to love every dying second.

He moaned and felt the pressure inside him building, climbing in no time at all. After all these years they'd known each other, it would be wrong for this to be over in thirty seconds flat, so he pulled her gently up to kiss her lips, and tried to slow things down.

"You're making me crazy, Mace."

"That's kind of the point."

He felt her smile as she kissed him again.

"I can definitely appreciate that, but I want to make this last," he said huskily.

"Lasting is a good thing if you can do it."

"Is that a challenge?"

"Maybe." She dragged her breasts over his flesh and he caught her up against him, stopping the friction but making the touch no less pleasurable. His hands moved lower to her perfect ass.

"I think I'm up to the challenge."

"Up?" Macey whispered. "Yes. Definitely." She groped him again to emphasize her point.

For the first time in months, Derek felt alive.

MACEY SUDDENLY FOUND herself flipped onto her back with Derek on top of her. She grinned to herself, knowing that this was finally going to happen. Based on the past few minutes, she was confident it would be the most amazing experience of her life. After so many years of wanting him, he was here in her bed, wild for her and making her absolutely frantic with need.

He took his time exploring her body and she let him, because every time she tried to return the favor, he held her wrists down and told her to let him do what he was doing. She didn't take much convincing. With everything he did to her, her need grew, to the point she was practically whimpering.

"Derek, please," she said.

He worked his way up to kiss her lips, and stared into her eyes in the darkness. "Please what?"

"You are a wicked man."

He grinned. "Wicked, huh?"

"Evil."

"All this attention I'm giving you and I'm evil?"

He held his body over hers, not quite touching. When she arched her back to get closer, he moved just out of her reach. After a few rounds of cat and mouse, Macey directed his body to the exact place she needed him.

"Protection?" he whispered, sounding as needy as she felt.

She closed her eyes for a second, insanely tempted to be careless and stupid and do without.

"Nightstand," she said. "Drawer."

After their run-in in this very bedroom a couple weeks ago, she'd bought a box of condoms. Not because she truly thought she and Derek would need them, but because she'd experienced firsthand how thoroughly she lost her mind when he touched her. It'd been a huge just-in-case purchase. One she enthusiastically applauded now.

He leaned over, opened the drawer, pulled out a packet and sheathed himself, taking no more than five seconds. It seemed like minutes.

Finally, he moved back on top of her, and Macey wrapped her arms around him, treasuring this moment, wishing it could last forever. Their eyes met as he entered her, and she was so full of love for him that tears blurred his image. She tried to memorize every one of his features, his expressions, the sounds he made, because this wasn't something that would happen again.

Derek whispered things to her—how beautiful she was, how good she felt. All of it made her melt a little more.

She ran her hands over him, loving the feel of his muscles, his strength, the hair at his nape, the angles of his face. Then she forgot about everything else as he pushed her higher and higher.

She held on to him as he took her to an intoxicating, amazing release. The sound of her name on his lips had a toe-curling effect, or maybe that was everything else he was doing to her body. Her heart expanded and over-flowed with her feelings for him.

Derek pressed kisses to her neck, her jaw, her lips, nibbling and teasing her. She held him tightly, with no intention of ever letting go. Their breathing gradually slowed and he rolled to his side, taking her with him, their bodies still entwined.

He seemed just as reluctant as she was to let it end.

"If I'd known all it took to get you in my bed was to nearly drown, I would've thrown myself in the sea ages ago," Macey said, unable to stop smiling.

His arms tightened around her. "Don't even say that. I was so damn scared when I saw your head go under out there…." Derek kissed her forehead and brushed her hair from her face. "I couldn't stand it if something happened to you."

"Nothing did. You came to my rescue. Shh, no more about that. Let's just enjoy this."

He chuckled. "*Enjoy* is one word for it. That was pretty damn amazing, woman."

"Not bad at all," she said, stifling the grin that wouldn't quit.

"Not bad?" He gripped her more tightly, taking her breath away. "Care to rephrase that?"

She laughed and tried to hold out, but then he tickled her at the waist. He was playing dirty, using info he'd had since they were kids to pinpoint her most ticklish spot. "The best."

He loosened his grip and kissed her. "That's more like it."

Macey burrowed into his chest, taking in his scent, his heartbeat, his coarse hair against her cheek. She couldn't remember ever feeling this content in her life.

"I love you, Dare," she whispered as she drifted toward sleep.

Not noticing that Derek's whole body tensed.

CHAPTER TWENTY-TWO

DEREK WAITED FOR Macey's breathing to even out before he slid from under her and took refuge in the bathroom. He cleaned up and put on his now-dry clothes, then returned to the bedroom and stared at Macey. She was asleep in the middle of the bed, the sheets tangled around her legs, leaving most of her body visible in the dim light.

He couldn't let her love him. Couldn't love her back. He'd been an idiot to get involved tonight, and the sad thing was that he'd known it going in, but hadn't cared. He'd been so bowled over he'd let the sex happen.

He should've left when she'd fallen asleep on the couch.

Regrets weren't going to do anyone a damn bit of good, so he turned and walked away, straight to her front door. He let himself out into the muggy night and made his way home to his condo and his dog, who looked up at him from his brand-new kennel as if Derek had let him down, too, by staying away so long.

Derek took Burnaby outdoors to relieve himself and set out food and water. Then he went to his mostly unused bedroom and sat on the edge of the bed. Julie stared at him from the frame on the nightstand and his heart pounded.

"I'm sorry, Jules," he whispered. "I made a big mistake."

IT WAS JUST BEFORE DAWN when Macey stirred. She stretched and felt sore muscles in places she didn't normally. Then everything about her mind-blowing night with Derek flooded back to her. She lazed there in the dark shadows, remembering, replaying their lovemaking in her mind like a movie. A very R-rated movie. It took several minutes to realize that Derek was no longer with her. That his side of the bed was cool and hadn't been slept in. She rolled to her stomach and came up on her elbows, trying to recall when he'd left. But she had no idea. He'd gone while she was sleeping, like someone who had major regrets about something he'd done.

She dropped her head to the pillow. She was a regret. The most magical night of her life and Derek regretted it.

No, that wasn't necessarily true. He might not have regretted it if she hadn't been dumb enough to tell him she loved him. Her mind had been hazy and she'd been about to drift off, but she'd been conscious of what she was saying. She'd meant to tell him she loved him.

So now here she was, alone.

She'd totally screwed up. Saying she loved him made it sound as if she had future plans with him, wanted more from him. Well, of course, in a perfect world she did.

But her world was far from perfect and she wasn't after anything more. She'd told him that earlier and meant it. She'd gone into last night knowing they wouldn't have a future together beyond friendship. Now it looked as if even that was ruined.

The pain she'd known would eventually hit her nearly knocked her out. Her eyes stung. She rolled over to her back to stare at the ceiling, unable to think of a single reason to get out of bed. Still naked, she shivered and bent to pull the twisted blankets up over her body.

It was time to go home.

MACEY CARRIED HER FEW possessions out to her neglected Corolla. Another wonderful part of island life— being able to walk just about everywhere. And having awesome scenery wherever she went.

She'd spent the past few hours packing and thinking about all the things she was going to miss about San Amaro Island. Well, almost all. She hadn't allowed herself to dwell on Derek for a single minute. It was going to hurt too badly and she didn't want to break down yet. Didn't have the energy to handle that much sadness. She had the entire eight-hour drive home to reckon with that.

Her body ached from her ordeal in the water the day before. Then she'd gotten only a few hours of sleep. And to wake up before the sun and face such a gargantuan screwup... She was running on autopilot, praying she'd make it through the drive.

The thought of staying here for another night, heck,

even another hour, made her want to weep. She couldn't stand to sleep in a bed that held so many memories. Every place on the island reminded her of Derek in some way. If she got sleepy on the drive home, she'd pull over and snooze for a few minutes.

"Hey, Macey." Evan came down the stairs a few seconds after her.

"Hi." She tried hard to sound normal.

"You're leaving?" he asked.

She nodded, her throat tightening enough that speaking wasn't advisable.

"I thought you were here for another week."

She swallowed and closed her eyes for a moment. "I have to go now."

"Let me open that." He took her keys and unlocked the trunk of her car, then lifted her suitcase inside. She was also carrying her pillow, and held it tightly to her chest. "You're okay from yesterday, though, right?"

Yesterday. Yesterday was Derek. Macey looked up in question at Evan.

"Derek said you nearly drowned. Are you okay?"

"Oh." *That.* "Yes. I'm fine." Absolutely great.

"Where *is* Derek?" Evan looked toward Macey's apartment door, then up and down the sidewalk lining the parking lot. She didn't follow his gaze. She knew Derek was nowhere near.

"He's… I don't know. At home. At work." She honestly couldn't remember if he was scheduled today. All she knew was that Andie had taken Macey's shift, for which she'd be eternally grateful.

Evan was staring too closely at her now. "What's going on, Macey? Something happened between you two, didn't it?"

The tears that had stalled out earlier were suddenly fighting to pour from her eyes. She nodded, studying the pavement in earnest.

"Did he do something to you?" Evan asked.

Macey quickly shook her head. "It's okay. He didn't do anything wrong." She sucked in a breath. "*I* did." She couldn't look at Evan. She was too close to losing it completely.

He reached out and squeezed her forearm. "Sorry to hear that," he said. "I would've put money on the two of you."

That was the breaking point, and her shaking shoulders gave away her silent sobs.

"Macey. It's okay…."

Evan didn't seem like the type who would handle a bawling woman well if it was his mother or sister, let alone some crazy temporary neighbor he'd taken on one date, only to have her admit to caring about another guy.

She nodded and forced a smile. "I know. Everything's okay." But her next breath was raspy and she laughed uneasily. Borderline hysterically. "Sorry. I'm a mess."

He drew her over to the parking lot curb and sat them both down. She pulled her pillow more snugly against her. The surrounding cars shielded them, so she no longer felt like a freak on display.

Macey bent over her pillow and hid her face in it, squinting her eyes and willing away the overwhelming need to cry some more. After a few seconds, she sucked in a slow, steadying breath and braced herself.

"Why would you think Derek and I would make it? We weren't together."

Evan shrugged. "Just got that vibe when I talked to him."

"You talked to him?" She'd sensed the tension between the two men so many times, and wondered what kind of a scene she'd missed.

"He stopped by the station."

"The fire station?"

"The fire station."

"What for?" Macey knew her eyes were bulging, but at least they'd stopped watering. If Derek was thinking about going back to firefighting, that'd be the best news....

"Just stopped by. I showed him around. The captain told him he'd love to have him."

"And Derek's response?"

"Noncommittal."

She refused to let that dampen her hope. Maybe he was making progress toward getting a life back. She'd have to call Andie periodically to check in and make sure he was okay, once she was back in Dallas. At this point it didn't seem likely she'd be able to call him directly.

"This is a lot to ask, especially after I cried all over you, plus messed up our date...." Macey bowed her head and laughed. "You must hate me, actually."

Evan laughed, too. "Strangely, no. What's a lot to ask?"

"Could you keep trying to convince Derek to join the department?"

"He won't listen to me."

"It'd have to be subtle, of course. If he knows you have an agenda and it comes from me, he'll just get mad."

"He won't be receptive to pressure. I'm not sure what all happened to him but I can tell it was heavy."

"It was." She nodded sadly, wishing there was a guaranteed way to lead Derek back to his career. "Maybe just…stop by the bar every once in a while? Even seeing you will force him to think about the fire department."

"That's a big favor you're asking. Stopping by a bar on the beach? I don't know…."

She hit his thigh, actually forgetting for a few seconds that her life had taken a turn for the worse. Then she checked her watch and realized it was later than she thought. "I need to go. Long drive ahead."

"You going to be okay all the way to Dallas?" he asked. "You seem pretty wiped out."

"I have to get away. I'll be fine."

"If I didn't have to work in the morning I'd drive you up there."

"Why are you so nice to me?"

He stared at her for several seconds. "No idea. Seems like the thing to do."

He stood and she did the same, then opened the door of her car.

"Thanks for everything, Evan. Today and before."

"It's nothing. If you come back to the island, be sure to look me up to say hello."

She nodded, tried to smile and got in the car. As she drove away, though, she was certain she wouldn't have a single reason to come back here.

"DID YOUR DOG KICK THE bucket or what?" Andie asked from behind Derek.

He whipped around, scowling. "What?" He glanced outside the bar to where he'd tied Burnaby. The pooch was lying in the shade of a tall enclosure that kept the Dumpster out of sight. "Dog's fine."

"Then I'm going out on a limb here and betting your mood is related to Macey's leaving the island."

"She doesn't leave till Saturday." Only a few days of avoiding her. It'd be a simple task if they didn't work together nearly every day. "Why isn't she working right now?" he asked, suddenly realizing Andie had opened in Macey's place.

Andie stared at him with an odd look on her face, a sympathetic half grin. "You don't know, do you?"

Derek wasn't in the mood to play a guessing game so he turned to the prep area and wiped it clean. From the sound of it, he didn't want to know whatever she was talking about.

"She's leaving, if not gone already. She called me to take several of her shifts. Kevin took the others. Everything's covered. Said you should mail her final paycheck to her mother's house in Dallas. I wrote down the address if you need it."

Derek had stopped scrubbing at the word *leaving*. Macey was leaving the island early? Without saying a word to him? The edginess that had been driving him all morning turned into full-out anger.

She couldn't just take off. She had a job here. He didn't care if she'd arranged to cover her shifts.... You didn't just bolt without notice.

He snapped the towel into the bucket in the corner, causing the water to splash up. "I'm going to stop her."

"You can't, Derek."

He glared at Andie. She didn't know what the hell she was talking about.

"You're the last person she wants to see."

That stopped him cold. He slammed his fist down on the metal refrigerator unit that served as the prep area, and let out a stream of curses at the intense pain to his hand. Several customers looked his way but he ignored them. Barely noticed them.

"She's probably already gone, anyway," Andie continued. "Nothing you can do now."

That was the truth, or part of it. The other part was that he *shouldn't* do anything about Macey.

"Probably a good thing she left early," he finally muttered.

"Ha. Keep telling yourself that."

Andie wandered nonchalantly to the back room, which practically made steam come out of Derek's ears. He wasn't kidding himself about anything anymore. The only time he'd done that was while he was in Macey's bed.

"Counter's dirty." Gus's gruff voice coming from the vicinity of his usual stool did nothing to soothe Derek.

"Clean it yourself," he retorted.

Instead of the bossy reply Derek expected, his uncle made his way behind the bar toward the bucket. Derek watched him pick up a towel and wring it out. It was a matter of minutes before Gus found out about Macey and laid into Derek for scaring her off.

"Hello, Andie-girl," Gus called out to the back room.

"Hey, Gus. Need a burger?"

"Believe I do. And some whiskey." The last bit he said to Derek, who thought he could use some hard stuff as well today.

Derek poured Gus's drink as his uncle wiped down half the bar counter. Watching the old man try to work, Derek felt like a jerk. "Give me that. Not your job anymore."

"I can still wipe down the bar," Gus said, but he surrendered the towel to Derek and took his place on his stool.

"Where's your woman?" Derek asked.

"Getting her hair cut and curled. Where's yours?"

"She died in a fire."

"Dammit, boy, I know about Julie and I'm sorry as hell." He took a gulp of whiskey. "You know damn well I'm talking about Macey."

"She's not my woman and she went back to Dallas."

"A bit early, isn't it?"

"Yep. I scared her off." He might as well confess—that was easier than hearing Gus spout off about how he'd messed up.

Gus studied him in uncharacteristic silence. Took another swallow. Then he nodded. "It's difficult."

"What's difficult?"

"Letting go. Knowing when to let go."

Derek moved to the bar and leaned on it, unwilling to have customers overhear their conversation.

"I know it's not the same, but I had a hell of a time letting go of this bar and everything it stood for. My independence. Ability to earn a living. Life outside the jailhouse, as I used to call the old folks' home."

"Not the same thing at all."

"Same thing, no. I already said that. But leaving one part of your life behind to move on to the next. Hate to tell you, but you do have to move on sometime, be it now or a year from now."

Andie brought out a basket with a burger and fries, and set it in front of Gus. "No pickles. Extra cheese. Tread lightly, this guy's in a black mood and I have to work with him all day."

She went outside to clean tables before Derek could say anything. Two customers approached the bar and Derek took their order, handed over their bottles of beer and collected their money as Gus watched him closely. Derek took his sweet time cleaning, restocking, checking the trash. More customers ambled in and he and Andie spent a good half an hour waiting on everyone. When it had calmed down again, Gus gestured him over.

"Tell me one thing," his uncle said. "Did things not work out between you and Macey because you don't have the right kind of feelings for her, or because of Julie?"

"It's only been six months since the fire."

Gus nodded. "So you do care about Macey."

"We're done with this conversation," Derek said, going to the ice machine to loosen the cubes from the sides.

"Might be, but it doesn't change the fact that you're throwing away the possibility for a good future because you can't let go of the past. Is that what Julie would want for you?"

"What time's the bus picking you up today, Gus?"

Wouldn't be soon enough.

It was the same old thing. Gus didn't understand. He'd never lost someone as Derek had. Couldn't understand that just flipping a switch and moving on wasn't the way it worked.

He was sure it'd been hard for Gus to accept his new lifestyle, but losing the bar wasn't remotely the same as losing a woman.

CHAPTER TWENTY-THREE

"Look at you, Macey!" Kathy Severson, Derek's mother, slid out of the booth at Grace's, the restaurant she and Macey's mom owned, and held out her arms for a hug. "You're tanned and beautiful."

Her tan had actually faded in the week she'd been back. "It's good to see you, Mrs. S. Hi, Mom."

"Hi, sweetie."

Mrs. Severson had just gotten back into town from a conference. Macey and her mom had been living under the same roof for seven days, but they'd hardly had a chance to catch up. Macey had kicked into high gear with her nonprofit foundation, working on grant proposals and soliciting support from local businesspeople during daytime hours. Her mom had been working nights because they'd had a manager quit and hadn't yet replaced him. This was the first time the three of them had had a chance to meet and catch up.

Macey slid in next to her mother and kissed her cheek. "Good to see you, stranger."

"You should slow down a bit," her mom said.

"Me?" She chuckled. "Hello, Pot. I'm Kettle. A much younger kettle than you, I might add."

"I'm fifty-one, my dear. Not quite ready to hang it up yet."

"As long as you take care of yourself," Macey said, studying the newish wrinkles on her mom's face up close.

"I'm doing great, honey. Quit worrying about me."

"You look good," she declared, but she'd never fully relax and believe the cancer wouldn't be back. The odds were low—it'd been almost fifteen years—but Macey wasn't willing to let her guard down.

"You look tired yourself," her mom replied.

Mrs. Severson perused Macey with a critical eye from across the small table. "You're right, Cheryl. She does. The tan covers it up from a distance, but, Macey, honey, you don't look so hot."

"Gee, thanks." She took a sip of the ice water in front of her. "I've been working my tail off all week, thank you."

"How's that going?" Derek's mom asked.

"Slower than I'd like, but I'm getting some substantial donations." She'd managed to secure about a third of her initial goal this past week, thanks in large part to one of her late father's friends, who'd given generously. She'd been successful with a handful of others as well, but on a smaller scale.

A waiter showed up at their table to take Macey's drink order. She noticed both women had glasses of red wine. "Could you have the bartender make me a custom drink?"

"If you can tell me what's in it, she can try. She's good," the waiter said.

"Better than good, Alberto. Deirdre's the best around." Mrs. Severson glanced toward the bar and raised her wineglass in salute when she caught the bartender's eye.

Macey asked to borrow Alberto's pen and wrote the ingredients and proportions on a cocktail napkin. She handed it to the waiter, who read the list to himself.

"Interesting concoction," he said.

"It's called a Sandblaster. The specialty drink of my favorite bar on San Amaro Island."

"Derek's bar," Mrs. Severson said as the waiter took the order to Deirdre.

"The Shell Shack," Macey agreed. "All the tourists have to try a 'Blaster."

"Is the bar doing okay?" Mrs. S. asked.

Macey nodded. "Really well, actually."

"You must've helped that along quite a bit. I can't believe Derek was up for it in the state he's been in."

"He's not exactly a businessman," Macey said, smiling wistfully as she remembered some of their discussions and arguments about the changes she'd implemented, including coming up with the now-famous Sandblaster.

"How's he doing?" her mom asked.

The question of the hour, and one that Macey wasn't sure she could answer. After more than a month together, she still wasn't sure how much he'd recovered or whether her presence had hurt or helped. "He needs to be fighting fires."

That much she was certain of.

"I can understand his hesitancy," her mom said.

"I can, too," Macey replied, "but he needs fire-fighting."

"You think he'll come back here?" Mrs. S. asked, startled.

Macey shook her head. "I don't know if he ever will. But he might join the fire department down there. He took a tour of the station before I left."

"Oh, Macey, that's fantastic!" she said. "You must've been such a help to him."

"Uh, no. I wish. I think I just made things worse."

"No, honey. There's no way you could make them worse," Mrs. Severson said. "You didn't see him before he left town."

Macey's mom nodded sympathetically. "I only saw him at the funeral, but he was like a robot. Just a body going through the motions."

"It was heartbreaking." Mrs. Severson gazed off into space, looking as if she could break down in tears any second. "You don't think he's doing any better now?" Macey wished she could tell her Derek was back to his old self. She seriously wished he was, worried mother or not.

Alberto set her drink in front of her. "Deirdre would like to know if she came close with this."

Macey took a long sip through her straw and closed her eyes. The island and everything she loved about it—the little shack bar, the waves, the smell of the sea,

Derek—it all came back to her with the single taste. "Perfect," she said. "She *is* the best."

Alberto nodded in satisfaction. He took their lunch orders and then left the three women alone.

"Derek's made a little progress," Macey said after another sip. "Andie said he never smiled or laughed before I came, but I think that changed. I forced him to do some touristy things with me."

"Bless your heart," Mrs. S. said.

Macey smiled sadly, remembering the dolphin cruise and how Derek had seemed to come alive for a couple of hours. Even though everything had since collapsed between them, the memories of that day were still magical.

"Macey, honey, what's going on? There's something you're not telling us. What's wrong with my son? Is it worse than I'm aware of?"

How did she tell her mom and Derek's what had happened…without actually spelling it out? "He's going to be okay," she said finally. "But I don't think he and I are still friends."

"What?" her mother said in shock. "You two have been close for so long. I don't believe for a minute that'll change."

Mrs. Severson was studying her critically. "What happened, honey?"

Macey squirmed. If she could disappear she would right now, gladly. "I…said some things I shouldn't have."

"Did you get fed up with him?" her mom asked. "Angry? Frustrated? Is that what happened?"

"Well…that happened plenty, but that wasn't what I was talking about."

"He found out how you feel about him," Mrs. Severson guessed.

"Wh-what do you mean?" Macey asked, suddenly sweating, even though the restaurant was well air-conditioned.

Derek's mom put her hand over Macey's on the tabletop. "I know how much you care about him. We've known for years," she admitted, glancing at Cheryl for backup.

"Since you two were little kids we've hoped that someday you'd end up together," her mom said.

"It started out as a selfish thing. We thought it would be neat to be in-laws of sorts. But then when you hit high school and had such a crush on Derek…"

Macey could have died of embarrassment. "What makes you think I had a crush on him?"

"Oh, honey, it was easy to see," Mrs. Severson said. "Of course, we were watching for it."

"Did Derek know?" she asked, terrified. If he'd known all this time that she was half in love with him… She couldn't stand to think about it.

But Mrs. S. was shaking her head. "That boy is my son and I love him like nothing else, but he *is* a male. He was oblivious, I'm quite certain."

Macey leaned against the back of the booth. Thank goodness.

"But now he knows," his mom continued, not really phrasing it as a question.

"I told him—" She broke off and stared at the mahogany tabletop and the deep green cloth napkin in front of her. "I'm so embarrassed. I said the *L* word."

Her mom put her hand on Macey's thigh and patted it.

"This is good," Derek's mom said, nodding slowly, thoughtfully.

"How much have you had to drink?" Macey asked her, glancing around for an empty wine bottle. This was anything *but* good.

"Something has to wake him up, and it sounds like you did that."

"No. All I did was scare him away."

"He didn't take your declaration well, huh?" Mrs. Severson asked.

"He took off. I never saw him again. That's why I came home early."

Both women nodded and she was thankful they didn't try to tell her she'd done the wrong thing.

"Some space might be wise," her mom said.

"He was no doubt surprised," his mom added.

"You guys don't get it, do you? I ruined it. He's still mourning Julie. He doesn't want anyone else and I just suffocated him by letting him know how I feel."

"Did you ask him if he loves you?"

"No way." That was the one thing she'd done right…. She'd let it go as soon as she'd, well, let it go. "The thing is the timing has never been right for us, and it never will be. I picked the worst possible moment to tell him."

Mrs. Severson shook her head adamantly. "I disagree, Macey. I think, at long last, the timing was exactly right. I liked Julie just fine and I wish like the dickens it hadn't ended like it did. But he's still alive, whether he's figured that out or not. He's got his whole life ahead of him. I just know he cares deeply for you. It may take him some time to give himself permission to move on, but when he does, I hope you're still there for him."

"He doesn't want to see me."

"Did he tell you that?"

"Not in words."

Nobody spoke, and the sounds of clinking dishes and conversation around them faded to nothing for Macey. When she turned her head toward her mother, she saw her head shaking slowly, as if Macey was the biggest disappointment ever. Macey looked over at Mrs. Severson, whose expression was unreadable.

"What?" Macey demanded.

There was a long hesitation before her mother spoke. "Didn't you go to the ends of the earth to become more confident, Macey?"

"You mean Thailand?" The question came from left field and Macey struggled to follow her mom's train of thought.

"Thailand. Yes. You told me you joined the Peace Corps, in part, to become more aggressive, less passive."

"Yeah...."

Her mom's eyes widened momentarily, as if to say, *Well?* Macey slowly grasped her meaning.

"You think I need to be more aggressive with Derek."

She'd *slept* with him. She couldn't be much more aggressive than that, could she?

"If you're comfortable leaving it where it is, then leave it. If you think you've done everything you can, then by all means, move on, my dear."

Alberto approached and set up a stand to put his large round tray on. Macey hardly noticed as he placed their meals in front of them.

She hadn't done everything she could where Derek was concerned. She'd thought she'd done more than she should, and because she was embarrassed, she'd taken off. Run away again. Been completely passive when it came to the single most important thing in her life.

"Macey, honey?" his mom said. "You okay?"

She shook her head. "I'm not comfortable leaving it where it is, actually. I have other things to tell him. I didn't say much of anything." She picked up her purse and slipped the strap over her shoulder. "You can have my sandwich for dinner tonight, Mom. I have something to take care of."

She slid out of the booth and bent to hug the other two.

"That's my girl," her mom said. "Call when you get to San Amaro, please. Be safe."

"Go get 'im," Mrs. S. said with touching determination.

Macey didn't know if she would "get him" at all, but she'd never been more sure in her life of one thing, and that was that she had to lay it all on the line and see what happened.

If he didn't have feelings for her, if he didn't want her in his life, then Derek was going to have to tell her to her face.

CHAPTER TWENTY-FOUR

THE WEATHER SUCKED. Business sucked. Derek stared out The Shell Shack doorway at the sheets of rain coming down. He could barely tell where the gulf started, it was so gray and wet outside.

The plastic over the windows was starting to fog up. They'd had only a handful of customers since opening; the rain had been alternating between downpour and drizzle all day, and it appeared no one wanted to venture out for a beer. It'd been a full week since Macey had left, and now that his anger had subsided, he... Dammit, he missed her. He still saw Julie's photo every night and he still felt like an insensitive bastard whenever he caught himself thinking about Macey instead of Julie.

The mugginess of the bar was getting to him. Sweat coated his body, even though outside was anything but balmy. It seemed as if oxygen was getting hard to come by in here.

"I'll be back later," he called out to Andie, who was behind the bar doing the *New York Times* crossword puzzle.

Derek left the shelter of the building and welcomed the sting of rain pelting him. It was easier to breathe out here, but something inside still clawed at him, drove him to do...something.

The beach was deserted as far as he could see. It took only seconds to become thoroughly drenched, but he couldn't care less. He headed down the concrete stairs to the sand and took off running toward the south.

The Shell Shack was closer to the north end of town and the developed part of the island. He'd had no intention of running all the way to the southern tip, but once he started, once his lungs began crying for relief, he didn't want to stop. The pain gave him something to think about besides the jumble in his brain.

His leg muscles shook as he ran past the fire station without a glance. He could see the southern end, made of a natural rocky pier, from here, and he knew he had to keep going until he got there. Once he reached it, he made his way over the slippery rocks, wet from the rain and splashing waves, to the very tip.

It was wild out here. Intense. The wind whipped him, and water crashed over the rocks just below. One good wave could easily drench the rock he sat on and wash him into the rough water.

Thunder clapped and lightning ripped through the evening sky. Normally the sun would still be shining, but the clouds were heavy and dark gray.

It was dangerous as hell out here. Derek knew that and didn't give a damn.

He briefly thought about what would happen if he was washed into the turbulent water. He'd likely be thrown against the rocks and die of a head injury…. How would Macey react if something happened to him?

He believed her when she'd said she loved him. He

didn't understand why she felt that way, but she wouldn't say it if it wasn't true.

Macey would experience the same pain he'd endured when Julie had died, he suddenly realized. It nearly bowled him over. He didn't ever want her to go through that. Especially not for him. *God.*

If he got hit by a bus or washed against rocks, it wouldn't make a damn bit of difference to Julie.

The truth hit him like a boulder to the head.

He was letting his life pass him by because of some misguided loyalty to Julie, but there was nothing left of Julie except memories. Loving Macey wouldn't destroy those memories. Nothing could destroy them.

The woman he'd loved, though, was gone.

Without a doubt, Julie would never want him to retreat from life, from Macey, out of some crazy concern for *her.* If their positions were reversed, he'd want Julie to go on. Get over him. Remember him and their good times, sure, but he would never expect her to live like a nun and sacrifice love. He'd want her to find happiness.

He stood up on the slippery rock, bracing himself against the wind. Goddammit, what had he done?

The wind gusted and he lost his footing. He threw his left leg out to a rock nearby, but it didn't stop his fall. He landed on his ass and a sharp edge dug into his lower back. His head hit another boulder, sending pain slashing through his skull. Derek thought for a minute he was going to die, but he was still conscious and the pain gradually subsided somewhat. He was still on the rocks, and damn lucky he hadn't ended up in the drink.

Yet. As he eased himself to a sitting position, the gravity of his position finally hit him. He needed to get off this jetty while he could.

He had to talk to Macey, to see if they had a chance.

Derek rolled over and started crawling, making his way across the treacherous rocks toward the relative safety of the wave-beaten shore. The jetty was about a hundred feet long, which hadn't seemed like much on the way out here. Now it stretched in front of him like a hundred miles.

The rain pelted his back and dripped down his face so that he could barely see what he was doing. As long as the rocks stretched in front of him, he figured he hadn't fallen into the gulf yet. He was doing okay.

He'd glanced back toward the tip, and realized he was only halfway to shore when the sounds of a siren reached him. A fire truck. His pulse quickened, an involuntary reaction, and he wondered what battle the guys were about to face.

Sixty seconds later, the wind carried a voice to him. "Stay where you are, sir. We're on our way."

What the…?

Derek wiped the water out of his eyes and squinted toward where the jetty met the shore. Holy hell. Three men were there, weighed down by all kinds of equipment. Firefighters. The rig was pulled up along the curb of the road that wound almost all the way down to the jetty.

It took Derek several long seconds to understand *he*

was the one they were yelling at. They were here to rescue *him*.

He didn't need to be rescued, dammit. He was one of them. A rescuer. Just like that, another piece of his life puzzle fitted into place.

He pulled himself up on a particularly smooth rock. "I'm okay!" he yelled. "I'll be there in a minute."

Or ten. Whatever. He was not going to let those guys climb out here on his behalf. Talk about humiliating.

He progressed a few feet, then raised his head again. "I'm a firefighter!" he called out to them. "I can make it."

He pushed himself to make faster progress. He was three-quarters of the way there now. He checked behind him again.

"Derek? Is that you?"

He couldn't recognize the man standing about ten feet out from the beach, not from this distance, with the rain coming down so hard. But he did know that voice.

"Evan. Stay there, man. I'm fine."

He kept going, ignoring the pain that centered in his head and ricocheted out into every part of his body. Soon he was close enough to hear Evan talking into his radio, although he couldn't understand what he was saying. It was undoubtedly best that way. He was sure they thought he was out of his mind.

"What the hell are you doing?" Evan asked when Derek was only a few feet away. The firefighter made his way toward him and grabbed his arm. "Can you stand up? Are you injured?"

"I'm fine," Derek said, and he pulled himself to his feet to appease Evan. Never mind that he couldn't have done it without someone to grab onto. "How did you guys know I was out there?"

"Saw some guy sprint by an hour ago and didn't think too much of it until we had a report of a lunatic out on the edge of the jetty, getting ready to jump."

"I wasn't about to jump. I may be crazy but I didn't want to kill myself."

"Could've goddamn fooled me," Evan muttered. "Scott is going to check you over. I don't care what you say."

They'd reached the end of the rocks at last, and together they climbed down to the stability of the sand. Clay and Captain Mendoza stood there watching him, presumably wondering what was wrong with him.

"Hey," Derek said, "sorry to concern you guys. Stupid move on my part."

"Do you have any injuries?" the captain asked him.

"Evan says he's going to sic the paramedic on me, so I might as well tell you I whacked my head on the rocks. Didn't lose consciousness. I feel fine." A small lie, but they didn't need to know his head felt as if it was split open. "I hope I haven't blown my chances for a job."

"We're going to get your head checked out before I make any promises," the captain said gravely. "If you've got any sense left, I imagine we'll take you."

Derek might have temporarily lost his mind, but he was as sure as he'd ever been about anything that he was ready to get back to work. He could pass any test the psychologists threw at him. The only thing left to settle was Macey, and whether she'd take him back or not.

CHAPTER TWENTY-FIVE

DEREK WAS READY TO CLIMB the walls after sitting around for a full hour. He'd let Scott Pataki give him an exam. Turned out he had a mild concussion from his fall and a couple of lacerations, but he hadn't even noticed he'd been cut until Scott pointed it out.

He was fine. All he wanted to do was get the hell out of here and track down Macey. He'd drive to Dallas tonight to do it. Didn't matter that it was dark and close to nine o'clock. He didn't want to waste another minute.

He left the station with a new job. Captain Mendoza hadn't questioned his sanity, after all. Had just nodded when Derek explained the walls had been closing in on him and he'd had to get out of the bar.

Unfortunately, he hadn't left the station on his own two feet. Captain Mendoza had insisted on giving him a lift in the station's SUV. Derek had told him to drop him off at The Shell Shack. He was glad to see Andie had closed up and gone home. The rain had slowed down but there was still no one out and about. Staying open would be a waste of time.

Derek made his way to his condo from the bar. He stuck to the street, walking along the curb. He'd had enough of sand and the beach for the day. Besides, he was in a hurry.

His head pounded when he tried to run, so he settled for a brisk walk. He'd refused any hard-core painkillers and planned to take a few Advil before he left.

He stuffed his hands in his pockets and felt for his keys. A smile broke out over his face when he grasped the goofy dolphin key chain he'd never had the heart to remove. He pulled it out and studied it, remembering Macey's determination to change his life with a cheap plastic souvenir. As he stared at it, he realized that bit by bit, she'd helped him see through the grief. She'd reminded him how to laugh. How to appreciate the beauty of the island. How to face up to the pain and make an effort to work through it.

He'd never been so damn glad to walk through the unlocked door into his condo. He might not need keys to get into his place, but he planned to keep the key chain as a reminder, no matter what happened with Macey.

He let Burnaby out of his kennel and scratched the dog's ears. Then he made his way back down the hall. He flipped the bedroom light on and whipped his damp shirt over his head as he entered the room; he'd refused dry clothes at the station. The shirt landed on the floor near the bathroom door.

Derek went straight to the photo of Julie and picked it up. He stared at it for several minutes and allowed himself to think about some of the best memories of her—the night they'd met at an off-campus party, the first time she'd taken him to Coneheads for ice cream, the first time she'd told him she loved him.

"I loved you, too," he said to the photograph. "Always

will. But I also love Macey. I think you'd be okay with that." He ran his finger over her hair, as if he could push it back from her face. "I won't forget you, Jules." He stared at her for several more moments, then went to his closet. He picked up the shoe box that had held his new tennis shoes. Wrapping the stiff tissue paper around the frame, he touched her lips one last time, then closed the lid. He put the box on the top shelf of the closet and closed his eyes for a few seconds, saying a silent goodbye to her.

He took in a deep breath and pushed it out hard, knowing, for the first time in a long time, he was doing the right thing.

Derek peeled off the rest of his clothes—his body was more tender than he'd thought—and climbed into a lukewarm shower. That and a truckload of caffeine were going to keep him awake until he was with Macey.

DEREK HAD JUST PULLED a pair of clean jeans on when the door to his condo flew open. Before he could react or wonder what was going on, he heard her voice. Had he lost his mind out there on that jetty?

"Derek?" Macey hollered. "Are you here? The bar is closed. Is everything all—"

He came out of the bedroom and she nearly walked right into him.

"—right?" She looked him up and down. "You don't have a shirt on."

"Uh, no. I don't."

"You're okay?"

"What are you doing here?" he finally asked, unable

to process it—that she was here in his condo, that she looked exhausted but somehow still beautiful, that she was commenting on something as mundane as his lack of a shirt.

She met his gaze. "I have some things to say and you're going to listen to me."

"Okay." He backed into his room and she followed him in. "Make yourself at home," he said drily.

Macey set her purse on his dresser, then crossed her arms as she looked at him. Stared at his chest, really, and he decided that not yet putting on his shirt was the best move he'd made all day.

"What is it, Mace? You're acting crazed."

"I *am* crazed. I've been on the road for eight and a half hours, because of you, even though you may not appreciate it. You may not even want to see me, for all I know, but that's just tough. Like I said, I have things to say to you."

Derek lowered himself to the bed and leaned against the wall, waiting. The less he said, the better the chances of her getting to the point.

"I told you I loved you, Dare, and I meant it. I know it sent you running, and I think I understand why. But at first, I was mad and hurt."

"I'm sorry, Mace—"

"Nope," she said, cutting him off. "My turn to talk. You get your turn after."

He'd never seen her quite like this, but she was sexy when she meant business.

She sat on the bed a distance from him. "I get that

you're still grieving for Julie. I never meant to belittle that. When I said I love you, it just sort of popped out, maybe not at a good time." She pulled her knee up under her and faced him. "All week long I regretted saying that."

"You shouldn't regret it," he said.

"I finally figured out something today."

"What's that?"

"That I'm not willing to give up just because you ran away one time."

He sat up straight. "Can I talk yet, Mace?"

She shook her head. "Let me get this out before I forget what I want to say."

He gestured for her to continue.

"I'm not trying to force you to forget about Julie. I know it's going to take you some time to get over what happened. But the thing is that…"

He saw her swallow, could tell she was running out of steam.

"What is it, Macey?" He held out his hand and she moved closer and took it.

"I've loved you for years, Dare." It took her a couple of seconds but she met his gaze. The love he saw in her eyes took his breath away.

"I didn't know…."

"So I'm not going to be pushed away just because I screwed up once and told you I love you when you're still trying to handle what happened last January. What I'm trying to say is that I'll wait for you to get through this. But only if there's any reason for me to wait. If you have any feelings for me at all…"

Derek leaned back against the wall in sheer, ecstatic relief. Macey watched him with uncertainty written all over her beautiful face. He pulled her close and held on to her, hoping to convey that he would never let her go. All the emotion of the day crammed into his throat, making it damn near impossible to say anything.

"Dare?"

He scooted back against the pillows and patted the spot next to him. She joined him, still waiting as he tried to figure out where to start.

"I'm so damn glad you came back," he finally said.

"Yeah?"

"Yeah. You saved me a long, lonely drive to Dallas tonight."

"What?" She craned her head to see his face better. "Why were you planning to go to Dallas?"

"I had a big day today. Ran down the beach like a lunatic, dared the storm to sweep me off the jetty, got rescued by the fire department, figured out how much I love you and need you in my life—"

"You fell off the jetty?" She rose up on her elbow, alarmed.

Derek ran his fingers through her hair, pushing it behind her shoulder, and shook his head. "No. Fell *on* the jetty, but that's not the point."

MACEY CLOSED HER EYES, trying to follow half of what he'd just said, when the last part of his sentence struck her. Her eyes popped open. "Did you just say...?"

"I love you and need you in my life."

Her heart felt as if it had exploded and spread warmth throughout her body. She stared hard into his eyes, took in the details of every last inch of his face. The planes and angles. The coarse hair beginning to shade his chin. His perfect lashes and the eyes that watched her intently.

Macey moved closer and kissed him full on the lips, not caring if she ever came up for air. He wrapped his arms around her and rolled to his back, pulling her on top of him.

For the first time, she kissed him with the knowledge that this wasn't stolen time, that she wouldn't live to regret it later. He hadn't explained exactly what had gone on in his head, traipsing around jetties and being rescued by firefighters, but all the explanation she needed, all the reassurance, was in the way he kissed her.

"I'm sorry I ran away," Derek finally said between kisses. "I felt so guilty making love to you when I was still trying to get over Julie's death."

"Shh. I understand."

He shook his head. "No, *I* understand. Finally. I was afraid to let myself live, since Julie couldn't anymore. I thought it was wrong to feel so good when I was with you…."

"Because Julie couldn't experience anything good anymore?"

He nodded. "I promise I won't bring her into our relationship all the time, but tonight I have to explain."

Macey nodded, running her finger along his jaw, wishing she could take away all his doubt and pain.

"It hit me that Julie wouldn't want me to give up my happiness because she died."

"You're right. She wouldn't. I didn't know her well, but I'm sure of that. She cared about you."

"I said my goodbyes less than an hour before you so calmly burst through my door. I packed her picture away. I don't want to get rid of it, Mace, but I don't need to see it every day. Don't want it between you and me."

"You and me," she repeated. "I like the sound of that."

"You better," he said, grinning.

"Oh yeah?"

"Yeah. I've been through a lot today to get to this point, right here, with you. You may not know this about me, but when I go after something, I tend to go all out."

Macey laughed. "I've known that since you were seven and decided you were going to build the world's tallest LEGO tower in the office at the restaurant."

"It would've set records," Derek said. "Wasn't my fault the ceilings were only nine feet high."

They laughed and kissed, until a thought finally burst through the cloud fogging up Macey's brain. She broke contact. "You're telling me that you figured all this out before I got here tonight?"

Derek nodded, his grin widening. "Yes, ma'am."

"So my whole speech that I was so determined to get out… I didn't even need to go there?"

He shook his head. "Not really. Though it definitely added to the moment. It was cute."

"Cute?"

"Endearing."

"Endearing?" Her voice rose.

"Sexy?" he ventured.

"I'll settle for sexy, I guess."

He pressed a kiss to her nose, then turned serious. "There's three more things we need to discuss," he said.

"Okay." She tried to sound confident, but his tone worried her.

"What do you think of living with a firefighter? I know it's not the easiest thing to ask—"

"You're going back?"

"I talked to Captain Mendoza tonight. I have to go through an interview and some other red tape, but then I can start as soon as I get some help at the bar."

"I'm so glad to hear that, Dare. It's who you are."

"It doesn't worry you?"

"It scares the crap out of me, but you're good. You'll do whatever it takes to come home to me every night."

"Got that right, woman. But…I need a manager for the bar. I don't suppose you know anyone with a background in running a small business?"

"I might know someone like that. As long as I can keep working on my foundation. I could start it up here instead of in Dallas. I don't think my donors would have a problem with that."

"You can do whatever you want as long as you're in my bed every night."

She shivered and closed her eyes. She'd waited so long

to hear something just like that from this man. It was almost surreal, but when she opened her eyes, he was still right there, inches from her face, his body melding into hers.

"You said three things," she whispered. "What's the last?"

He looked into her eyes. "This isn't a temporary thing for me. I don't know how long I've loved you, but I know no one has ever made me feel the way you do. Will you marry me, Macey?"

Giddiness and love made her feel lighter than air. "I, for one, have loved you just about forever," she said, grinning like crazy. "It's about time you saw the light."

Derek laughed. "I propose to a woman and all she can do is mention how dense I am." He pulled her close again and breathed in the scent of her hair. "Can you handle such an unenlightened man? Forever?"

"Absolutely. I'm looking forward to the challenge. Every single wonderful day of it."

* * * * *

*Be sure to read Evan Drake's big surprise
in the second book of Amy Knupp's*
THE TEXAS FIREFIGHTERS *miniseries,
on bookshelves in August 2010
wherever Harlequin Books are sold.*

LARGER-PRINT BOOKS!

GET 2 FREE LARGER-PRINT NOVELS PLUS
2 FREE GIFTS!

◆ HARLEQUIN®

Super Romance®

Exciting, emotional, unexpected!

YES! Please send me 2 FREE LARGER-PRINT Harlequin® Superromance® novels and my 2 FREE gifts (gifts are worth about $10). After receiving them, if I don't wish to receive any more books, I can return the shipping statement marked "cancel." If I don't cancel, I will receive 6 brand-new novels every month and be billed just $5.44 per book in the U.S. or $5.99 per book in Canada. That's a saving of at least 13% off the cover price! It's quite a bargain! Shipping and handling is just 50¢ per book.* I understand that accepting the 2 free books and gifts places me under no obligation to buy anything. I can always return a shipment and cancel at any time. Even if I never buy another book from Harlequin, the two free books and gifts are mine to keep forever.

139/339 HDN E5PS

Name _____ (PLEASE PRINT) _____

Address _____ Apt. # _____

City _____ State/Prov. _____ Zip/Postal Code _____

Signature (if under 18, a parent or guardian must sign) _____

Mail to the Harlequin Reader Service:
IN U.S.A.: P.O. Box 1867, Buffalo, NY 14240-1867
IN CANADA: P.O. Box 609, Fort Erie, Ontario L2A 5X3

Not valid for current subscribers to Harlequin Superromance Larger-Print books.

**Are you a current subscriber to Harlequin Superromance books
and want to receive the larger-print edition?
Call 1-800-873-8635 today!**

* Terms and prices subject to change without notice. Prices do not include applicable taxes. N.Y. residents add applicable sales tax. Canadian residents will be charged applicable provincial taxes and GST. Offer not valid in Quebec. This offer is limited to one order per household. All orders subject to approval. Credit or debit balances in a customer's account(s) may be offset by any other outstanding balance owed by or to the customer. Please allow 4 to 6 weeks for delivery. Offer available while quantities last.

Your Privacy: Harlequin Books is committed to protecting your privacy. Our Privacy Policy is available online at www.eHarlequin.com or upon request from the Reader Service. From time to time we make our lists of customers available to reputable third parties who may have a product or service of interest to you. If you would prefer we not share your name and address, please check here. ☐

Help us get it right—We strive for accurate, respectful and relevant communications. To clarify or modify your communication preferences, visit us at www.ReaderService.com/consumerchoice.

HSRLP10R

COMING NEXT MONTH

Available August 10, 2010

HARLEQUIN®

A Romance

FOR EVERY MOOD™

Spotlight on
Heart & Home

Heartwarming romances
where love can happen
right when you least expect it.

See the next page to enjoy a sneak peek
from Harlequin® American Romance®,
a Heart and Home series.

Five hunky Texas single fathers—five stories from
Cathy Gillen Thacker's LONE STAR DADS *miniseries.*
Here's an excerpt from the latest, THE MOMMY PROPOSAL
from Harlequin American Romance.

"I hear you work miracles," Nate Hutchinson drawled. Brooke Mitchell had just stepped into his lavishly appointed office in downtown Fort Worth, Texas.

"Sometimes, I do." Brooke smiled and took the sexy financier's hand in hers, shook it briefly.

"Good." Nate looked her straight in the eye. "Because I'm in need of a home makeover—fast. The son of an old friend is coming to live with me."

She was still tingling from the feel of his warm palm. "Temporarily or permanently?"

"If all goes according to plan, I'll adopt Landry by summer's end."

Brooke had heard the founder of Nate Hutchinson Financial Services was eligible, wealthy and generous to a fault. She hadn't known he was in the market for a family, but she supposed she shouldn't be surprised. But Brooke had figured a man as successful and handsome as Nate would want one the old-fashioned way. *Not that this was any of her business...*

"So what's the child like?" she asked crisply, trying not to think how the marine-blue of Nate's dress shirt deepened the hue of his eyes.

"I don't know." Nate took a seat behind his massive antique mahogany desk. He relaxed against the smooth leather of the chair. "I've never met him."

"Yet you've invited this kid to live with you permanently?"

"It's complicated. But I'm sure it's going to be fine."

Obviously Nate Hutchinson knew as little about teenage

boys as he did about decorating. But that wasn't her problem.
Finding a way to do the assignment without getting the least
bit emotionally involved was.

Find out how a young boy brings Nate and Brooke
together in THE MOMMY PROPOSAL,
coming August 2010 from Harlequin American Romance.